SPIRITUALITY AND BEYOND

EMBRACING THE INFINITE
JOURNEY WITH SHORT STORIES

ARNAB BASU
DR. N.SRIVIDYA

*Oh, angel sent from up above
You know you make my world light up
When I was down, when I was hurt
You came to lift me up*

*Dedicated to people who are trying to get in to the path of
Spirituality*

Contents

Contents

Acknowledgements

We would like to express my deepest gratitude to the pillars of my life: my family, my institution, and the divine guidance that has shaped my journey.

First and foremost, We owe an immeasurable debt of thanks to our family. Their unwavering support, love, and encouragement have been the foundation upon which I have built my aspirations and accomplishments. They have always believed in me, even when I doubted myself, and their sacrifices have enabled me to pursue my dreams with confidence and determination. To my parents, siblings, and loved ones, your strength, wisdom, and presence in my life are beyond words.

We also profoundly grateful to my department MBA & Institute of Engineering and Management (IEM), Kolkata, for providing me with an environment of growth, learning, and opportunity. The institution's ethos of excellence and innovation has instilled in us the desire to contribute meaningfully to society, pushing boundaries while upholding integrity. We proud to be a part of the IEM (affliated to University of engineering and management, Kolkata) community and thankful for the experiences that have enriched my academic journey.

Finally, We offer our heartfelt thanks to God, whose divine presence has been a constant source of strength, inspiration, and guidance throughout my life. It is through faith, surrender, and seeking inner wisdom that we have found peace in moments of uncertainty and clarity in times of doubt. God's guidance has been the compass that has steered me in the right direction and illuminated our path with hope and purpose.

Prologue

The journey inward is the profound exploration of the self, transcending external distractions to reconnect with the truth, wisdom, and connection within. In a world obsessed with external achievement, we often find ourselves unfulfilled, sensing that something deeper is missing. This longing sparks the journey—a quest to answer life's biggest questions not through external pursuits, but through the depths of our own consciousness. It is a path of awakening, requiring courage, patience, and the shedding of ego and illusion. The journey inward leads us to discover our true essence and our inherent connection to all of life.

Introduction: The Journey Inward

The journey inward is the profound exploration of the self that transcends external distractions, pointing us back to the deep wellspring of truth, wisdom, and connection that resides within all of us; it is a path that begins with a simple but profound question—Who am I?—and stretches through the labyrinth of our consciousness, guiding us to discover not only the essence of our being but our inherent connection to all of life, the universe, and the divine. In our fast-paced, hyper-connected world, where outer achievement is often seen as the ultimate measure of success, we find ourselves caught in the ceaseless cycle of pursuit—pursuit of wealth, validation, fame, status, and pleasure—as if these things alone will bring us happiness, peace, or fulfilment. Yet, despite reaching the milestones we set for ourselves, many of us are left with an underlying sense of dissatisfaction, an unsettling feeling that something vital is missing from our lives, something intangible and deeper than material success or fleeting pleasure. This sense of longing, often unspoken, becomes the first spark that ignites the journey inward: recognition that the answer to life's biggest questions—Who are we? What is our purpose? What is the nature of existence?—are not to be found in the external world, but within our own consciousness, in the quiet depths of our own soul. This realization calls us to look beyond the surface of our thoughts, emotions, and external circumstances and venture into the heart of who we are, shedding the layers of ego, conditioning, and illusion that obscure our true nature. The journey inward is not a linear path, but rather a winding road of awakening—a path that requires courage, patience, and the willingness to let go of old identities and beliefs that no longer serve us.

It begins with self-awareness, the ability to observe our thoughts, feelings, and actions without judgment, recognizing that we are not defined by them but that they are merely transient phenomena arising in consciousness, like clouds passing through a vast, open sky. Through the cultivation of mindfulness and presence, we come to realize that we are not the sum of our fears, desires, or past experiences, but something far more expansive: we are the awareness in which all these experiences arise and pass away. As we go deeper into our own consciousness, we encounter moments of stillness and silence where the noise of the mind begins to quiet, and in that silence, we find the clarity to see that we are not separate from the universe but intrinsically woven into the fabric of existence itself. In this profound stillness, we encounter the truth of our own being—the divine spark within that connects us to all life, to the source of creation, to the oneness that underlies the multiplicity of the world. The journey inward is not about becoming something we are not, but about unlearning the illusions that obscure our true essence, letting go of the false beliefs that bind us to fear, suffering, and separation. It is about surrendering the need to control, allowing life to unfold with grace and trust, and recognizing that we are not isolated individuals but expressions of a greater whole, part of an interconnected web of existence that stretches across time, space, and consciousness. As we awaken to the deeper layers of our being, we discover that the answers we seek—answers to the nature of life, the universe, and our own purpose—are not found through external means, but through the cultivation of an inner, direct knowing that transcends the limitations of the rational mind. The inward journey is a process of peeling away the layers of illusion, of confronting and releasing the fears, wounds, and attachments that have kept us bound to a limited sense of self, and embracing the vastness of who we truly are—a limitless, eternal presence, one with the divine, connected to all beings, and alive with the energy of the universe. It is a journey of transformation, where each step brings us closer to the truth of our own divine nature, a truth that transcends the boundaries of time, space, and form, and reveals to us the timeless reality of love, peace, and oneness that is the very fabric of existence itself.

As we embark on this journey, we discover that there is no final destination—no point at which we arrive, but rather an on-going unfolding, a deepening awareness, and an ever-growing recognition that the path itself is the destination, and the destination is not outside of us, but within. The inward journey is not just an individual path but a collective awakening, a movement toward the realization that all life is sacred, that we are all interconnected, and that our purpose is to awaken to the love, wisdom, and unity that bind us all together. In this journey, we learn that the universe is not something outside of us, but something we are deeply a part of, and that our greatest spiritual awakening lies not in escaping the world, but in embracing it fully, with an open heart and a deep sense of reverence, compassion, and love. Through this journey, we come to understand that spirituality is not a belief system or a set of practices, but an on-going experience of connection, transformation, and awakening to the deeper truth that we are not separate from the divine, but expressions of it—infinitely unique, yet part of a greater whole that transcends the limitations of time, form, and individuality. The inward journey is the ultimate return to the truth of who we are, and as we take each step, we find ourselves coming closer not just to the essence of our own being, but to the essence of all that is—connected, whole, and alive with the eternal, infinite presence of the divine

ONE

THE ESSENCE OF SPIRITUALITY BEYOND BELIEFS

Spirituality, when stripped of its external trappings and superficial layers, emerges as a profound, intimate exploration of the deepest essence of being, a journey into the heart of existence itself. It is a quest not for new doctrines or external validations but for an experiential understanding of life as it truly is, beyond the mind's constant narratives and the ego's endless pursuits. This journey is universal, an innate calling within every human soul, though it manifests differently across cultures, religions, and traditions. At its core, spirituality is not a set of beliefs to be memorized or rituals to be followed, but a transformative process that invites us to peel away the illusions of separation and discover the deeper truths of our interconnectedness with the universe, with all life, and with the divine.

Spirituality is fundamentally a process of unlearning—a deconstruction of the false identities we have created through years of conditioning, culture, and personal experiences. It asks us to move beyond the mental constructs that define us—the roles we play, the labels we carry, and the ideologies we hold—and to reconnect with the pure awareness that lies beneath all of them. In this state of unknowing, we begin to realize that our true nature is not limited by the body, the intellect, or even our individual experiences. Instead, it is vast, boundless, and timeless, a reflection of the infinite consciousness that underlies all of reality. This awareness does not come through intellectual comprehension or the acquisition of knowledge, but through direct experience. It is a knowing that arises from within, from a place that transcends duality, a space where the distinctions between self and other, between observer and observed, begin to dissolve. In this sacred space, we come to understand that the ultimate truth of spirituality is not something external to be attained, but an inner recognition of who we have always been. The divine, or whatever term one uses to describe the Source of all life, is not distant or separate from us; it is within us, in every cell, every breath, every moment. It is the very ground of our being, present in the stillness of our hearts, the silence of our minds, and the vastness of our consciousness. The practice of spirituality, therefore, is not about adherence to a set of beliefs or systems, but about living in alignment with this deeper truth. It is about awakening to the divine within, to the recognition that our individual consciousness is not separate from the collective consciousness of all beings, and that we are each a unique expression of the same universal Source. While belief systems—whether religious, philosophical, or metaphysical—serve as tools to help us navigate the mysteries of life, they are, at best, only stepping stones to a direct encounter with the divine. Beliefs can guide us toward deeper understanding, but they are not the ultimate truth. Spirituality, in its purest form, is about going beyond belief—about letting go of the need for certainty and moving into the realm of direct experience. It is in this realm that true transformation occurs. As we transcend our attachment to mental concepts, we awaken to the profound mystery and beauty of life, a mystery that cannot be contained within the narrow confines of words, doctrines, or philosophies. Here, in this place of unknowing, we experience the boundless love, peace, and clarity that is the essence of the divine, a love that transcends all understanding and unites us with all of existence. In this state of spiritual awakening, there is no longer a sense of separation between the individual and the universe.

The distinction between subject and object, between "I" and "you," begins to dissolve, and we realize that we are all interconnected, each of us an expression of the same Source. This awareness of interconnectedness is the foundation of true spirituality. It calls us to live with compassion, kindness, and humility, understanding that every being, every creature, and every atom of the universe shares in the same sacred essence. In the light of this realization, the ego's tendency to build walls of separation based on race, culture, or belief system begins to fade, replaced by a deeper understanding that we are all part of the same divine tapestry. The essence of spirituality, then, is a shift in consciousness, a transformation in how we perceive ourselves and the world around us. It is the journey from the false sense of self—the ego, bound by the limitations of thought and desire—toward the recognition of our true, boundless nature. This recognition is not an intellectual exercise; it is an awakening to a truth that is already present within us. It requires a deep level of surrender, the letting go of the mind's need to control, and openness to the unknown, to the vast, uncharted territories of consciousness. In this surrender, we find the freedom to be who we truly are, to live in alignment with the divine, and to express that divinity through our thoughts, words, and actions. In many ways, this process of spiritual awakening can be likened to a return to our original state, a remembering of who we are at our deepest level. It is a return to innocence, to purity, to the untainted awareness that existed before we were conditioned by society, culture, and personal experiences. It is a reawakening to the divine presence that has always been within us, a recognition that the sacred is not something separate from our everyday lives, but is woven into every moment, every experience. The external world, often perceived as mundane or even hostile, is, in truth, a reflection of the divine, and it is through our spiritual awakening that we learn to see this divine presence in all things. This recognition transforms how we live in the world. We begin to approach life with reverence and gratitude, seeing every encounter, no matter how small or seemingly insignificant, as an opportunity to connect with the divine. We also begin to realize that our actions, no matter how simple, have a profound impact on the world around us. In this way, spirituality becomes not only a path of inner awakening but also a call to act with integrity, compassion, and love in every aspect of our lives. As we deepen our understanding of spirituality, we come to realize that it is not a destination to be reached but an on-going process of unfolding, of peeling away the layers of illusion and returning to our true nature. It is not something we achieve or accumulate, but something we awaken to—something that has always been within us, waiting to be recognized. The essence of spirituality, then, is not found in beliefs, practices, or rituals, but in the direct experience of the divine, in the recognition that we are not separate from the Source of all life but are, in fact, one with it. The journey of spirituality is not about seeking something outside of ourselves, but about rediscovering what has always been present within. It is a journey of liberation—liberation from the ego, from the limitations of the mind, and from the belief in separation. It is the journey of returning to the truth of who we are—unlimited, eternal, and one with the divine.

ﭢﭢﭢ

Let us see a short story related to this.

There was a very good king who admires drawing and artists. He used to encourage several artists with huge donations for their art. One day, he wanted Bhagavadgita picture where Sri Krishna preaches Arjuna to be painted in his bedroom. He wished to have a first glance of Bhagavan Srikrishna and Arjuna on chariot, Krishna preaching Bhagavadgita to Arjuna.

He announced his decision in the majestic hall and he called for very famous and reputed artists to paint the picture. After several rounds of scrutiny, finally two people were selected to draw the picture on the wall. Two walls are selected just opposite to each other in the bedroom of the king. The king decides the best picture and artist after watching their painting. Six months' time is allotted to both the artists and all their needs are borne by the king himself. At the end of the allotted time, the king along with a panel of experts would examine both the paints and reward the best artist enormously. No one would disturb them during the period so that artist can focus on their job meticulously.

The first artist used to paint the picture very meticulously with wonderful mixture of colours as if both Krishna and Arjuna are alive. The second artist took a piece of glass

and rubbed the wall continuously throughout the day. Six months passed. On the final day, the panel members entered the room and examined the first painter and his drawing. It was a really beautifully drawn picture. Now, the chance is for the second one. The moment they opened the curtain, they could find themselves on the wall. They are spellbound. They thought without using any external tools such as paints, colours, brush, he could paint not on the wall, but inside the wall. Ultimately, the second one got the best prize.

In the similar line, we all have everything the ultimate happiness within ourselves itself. But not knowing this, we run outwards to grab or attain something to be happy. But this is a vicious circle. We will never be happy even after attaining that as there is no limit to desires. **JUST MOVE INWARDS. The Journey Inward**

Courtesy: Paramartha Kathalu by Swami Vidya Prakashananda Giri Swamy

TWO

THE NATURE OF CONSCIOUSNESS: A DEEPER UNDERSTANDING

Consciousness, that elusive quality of awareness that makes us aware of our thoughts, experiences, and the world around us, has long been the subject of philosophical inquiry, scientific exploration, and spiritual contemplation. For centuries, consciousness has been considered one of the greatest mysteries in human existence, a phenomenon that we experience intimately, yet fail to fully grasp. At its most basic level, consciousness is the faculty that allows us to perceive, reflect, and respond to stimuli, but it is far more than a simple function of the brain or a by-product of neural processes. It is the lens through which reality is filtered, the canvas upon which our lives are painted, and the ground of all experience. To explore the nature of consciousness is to delve into the very heart of existence, for consciousness is not just something we possess, but something that defines who we are and how we relate to the world. Consciousness shapes our perception of self, others, and the universe at large, and it informs how we interpret meaning, experience emotions, and make decisions. It is, in essence, the field of awareness within which the entirety of our life unfolds, a mysterious yet ever-present quality that eludes a full intellectual understanding. Despite its central role in our lives, consciousness remains, to many, an enigma—its true nature, origin, and purpose still not fully understood. While science has made significant strides in mapping the brain's functions and understanding neural activity, it has yet to explain how these physical processes give rise to the subjective experience of *being*, or the rich inner world of thoughts, feelings, and awareness. This gap, known as the *hard problem of consciousness*, persists, challenging both neuroscientists and philosophers alike. No matter how much we learn about the mechanics of the brain, the question remains: What is the true nature of consciousness itself? Some argue that consciousness is merely an emergent property of complex systems, a by-product of the brain's intricate activity. Others contend that consciousness is fundamental to the fabric of reality, suggesting that it is not something that arises from the physical world, but rather something that precedes or pervades it. The former perspective ties consciousness to the material world, while the latter posits that consciousness is the very basis of existence, an eternal, all-encompassing presence from which all things emanate.

To move beyond the confines of these opposing views is to realize that the true nature of consciousness cannot be fully understood through the intellect alone; it must also be experienced directly. Consciousness, at its most profound level, is not merely a function of the brain or a product of sensory inputs; it is a field of awareness that transcends time, space, and individuality. In many spiritual traditions, this deeper aspect of consciousness is referred to as *pure consciousness* or *universal consciousness*, a state of awareness that exists beyond the limitations of the body and mind, a boundless field of awareness that encompasses all of existence. It is in this deeper state that we find the answer to the age-old question of *Who am I?* For in this state, we realize that our individual consciousness is not separate from the universal consciousness, but rather a localized expression of it. The boundaries that we perceive between ourselves and others, between subject and object, between the self and the world, begin to dissolve. In this realization, we come to understand that consciousness is not an isolated phenomenon, but an interconnected, dynamic force that flows through all beings and all things. It is the medium through which life experiences itself, the source of all perception, and the bridge between the physical and the spiritual realms. This is where the exploration of consciousness begins to take on spiritual significance. Consciousness is not simply the ability to perceive; it is the ground of all existence, the container of all experience. In many mystical traditions, this understanding of consciousness is described as *the One, the Source,* or *God*—the infinite and eternal presence that underlies and sustains all things. Far from being a passive observer of reality, consciousness is seen as the creative force of the universe, the force that not only perceives, but also *creates* through perception. Everything that we experience, from the smallest particle to the vastest galaxies, is born from consciousness and exists within it. The human mind, often caught in the limited perspective of the ego, perceives itself as separate from the rest of existence. Yet, the deeper we go into the nature of consciousness, the more we realize that the sense of separation is an illusion, a construct of the mind that masks the underlying unity of all things. True spiritual awakening, therefore, is not about acquiring new knowledge, but about awakening to the awareness of oneness—recognizing that our individual consciousness is not separate from the universal consciousness, but one with it. This recognition brings about a profound shift in perception, a transformation that radically alters how we experience the world. No longer are we bound by the confines of ego and limited perspective; instead, we begin to perceive life through the lens of universal consciousness, seeing beyond the superficial differences that divide us, and recognizing the interconnectedness of all beings. This awareness not only transforms how we see the world, but how we live in it. We begin to act with greater compassion, empathy, and love, understanding that every action, every thought, and every intention ripples through the fabric of reality, influencing the whole. The realization of the unity of consciousness has profound implications for the way we live our lives, for it teaches us that we are not isolated individuals, but integral parts of a greater whole. In recognizing our oneness with all that is, we are called to live in harmony with the earth, with each other, and with the divine presence that pervades all existence. To truly understand the nature of consciousness is to recognize that we are both the experiencer and the experience itself, both the creator and the creation. In this state of awareness, we cease to be defined by the limited sense of self that arises from the ego, and instead come to recognize our identity as infinite and eternal—an expression of the divine, both unique and universal at once. As we deepen our understanding of consciousness, we begin to realize that it is not something that can be grasped or understood through thought alone, but something that must be experienced directly, through the silence of the mind and the stillness of the heart. In this stillness, we encounter the vastness of consciousness, the boundless space of awareness in which all things arise and dissolve. The nature of consciousness, then, is not confined to the material world or the individual mind; it is the very ground of being, the source of all creation, and the ultimate reality. It is both the path and the destination—the journey and the goal. To explore the nature of consciousness is to explore the depths of our own being, and in doing so, we come to realize that the true self is not the limited, individual ego, but the infinite, universal consciousness that pervades all of existence. This recognition opens the door to true freedom—a freedom that transcends the limitations of the body, the mind, and the ego, and aligns us with the eternal, unchanging presence that lies at the heart of all things. As we awaken to the deeper nature of consciousness, we come to understand that it is not just a part of our lives, but the very essence of our lives, the force that animates and sustains all that is. The nature of consciousness, when truly understood, reveals the interconnectedness of all beings and all things, and invites us to live in harmony with the universe and the divine presence that permeates all creation. In this understanding, we find the key to spiritual awakening and the ultimate liberation of the soul.

ᤧᤧᤧ

Let us watch a short story related to this topic.

There is a Guru (Teacher) who used to teach his disciples in his own house keeping them in his house all the time. It is like a residential school now a days. The disciples stay with their Guru and do whatever the Guru or his wife demands, including house chores. He has one disciple with him and later on another disciple joined them staying with them only.

One day, after having lunch, Guru wanted to take a small nap. Usually, the older disciple used to massage Gurus feet. While the disciple is about to start massaging, the second disciple, who joined lately, raised an objection that he used to do all these things for a long time. Hence, now it is his turn now to massage his feet. He pleaded Guru to grant him this task for this time.

The first one countered that he has a long experience in massaging the feet and the new disciple lacks it. So, it may cause inconvenience to Guru and asked him to let continue him only to do the massage. Both started quarrelling.

The Guru was in fix now and he thought of an action that would solve this problem. He told as he has two legs, they can massage one leg each. They agreed happily and they stared massaging the leg allotted to them. While massaging one leg has touched the other leg a little bit. The respective disciple got angry and shouted that "Why has your leg kicked my leg?" and he thrashed the other leg bitterly. The first one responded and he too kickd the other leg with a stick. This has progressed in to a huge quarrel. Guru woke up from sleep only to realise that his legs are paining a lot and those two disciples are thrashing the legs with sticks.

Immediately, he shouted to stop the nonsense and asked them to leave. They replied that it is their domestic affair and they need to finalise whose leg is better and greater. Guru retorted that they are his legs and the disciples are massaging Guru's legs, not their own legs. Hence, the question of which one is better and greater would not arise.

In the similar lines, we are all creatures are integral part of Universe and the Supreme. But we all forget this and we quarrel among ourselves to establish that we are better and greater than all others. If we can think beyond these divisions such as I and You, we all can live happily and rejoice, without competing with each other. Hence, **Live Beyond Beliefs of YOU and I.**

Courtesy: Paramartha Kathalu by Swami Vidya Prakashananda Giri Swamy

THREE

THE MIND-BODY CONNECTION: BRIDGING THE PHYSICAL AND THE SPIRITUAL

The mind-body connection is one of the most profound and essential aspects of human existence, a dynamic relationship that profoundly shapes our experience of the world, our physical health, and our spiritual growth. At the heart of this connection lies the understanding that the mind and body are not separate entities, but rather two dimensions of the same reality, intricately woven together into a unified whole. This connection manifests in countless ways, from the way our thoughts influence our physical health to the ways our physical state affects our emotional and mental well-being. Modern science has made significant strides in understanding this connection, particularly in fields like neurobiology, psychology, and psychoneuroimmunology, which study how mental and emotional states can influence the immune system, hormone production, and overall physical health.

For instance, research has shown that chronic stress, anxiety, and negative emotions can contribute to a wide range of physical ailments, including heart disease, digestive issues, and even cancer. Conversely, positive emotions such as love, gratitude, and joy can improve immune function, reduce inflammation, and promote healing. But the mind-body connection goes beyond the physical; it is also deeply tied to the spiritual dimensions of our being. In many spiritual traditions, the mind and body are seen as the two primary vehicles through which the soul experiences the world. The mind, often associated with consciousness and thought, serves as the interface between the external world and the internal self, while the body is the vessel through which we engage with the physical realm. Together, they form a bridge between the material and the spiritual, offering a means of experiencing, interpreting, and evolving within the vast complexity of existence. The idea that the mind and body are intimately connected has been a central theme in Eastern philosophies for thousands of years, particularly in traditions like yoga, Taoism, and traditional Chinese medicine. These traditions emphasize the importance of balance between mind, body, and spirit, understanding that each dimension influences the others. In yoga, for instance, the practice of asanas (physical postures) is designed not only to promote physical health but also to calm the mind, cultivate spiritual awareness, and ultimately unite the practitioner with their higher self. Similarly, meditation, an essential aspect of many spiritual practices, is seen as a tool for quieting the mind, connecting with the deeper realms of consciousness, and accessing spiritual wisdom. In these traditions, the mind and body are not seen as separate or competing forces, but as complementary aspects of a greater whole, each contributing to the individual's overall health, growth, and awakening. However, even in modern Western science, there is growing recognition of the importance of the mind-body connection, especially when it comes to healing. The placebo effect, where patients experience real physiological improvements after receiving a treatment they believe will help them—even when that treatment has no active ingredients—demonstrates the power of the mind to influence the body. Similarly, the practice of mindfulness meditation has been shown to have profound effects on physical health, reducing stress, improving heart health, and even altering the structure of the brain. This growing body of research points to the fact that the mind is not merely a passive observer of the body, but an active participant in shaping the physical experience. But to fully understand the mind-body connection, we must also consider the role of energy in this equation. Many spiritual traditions speak of the body as being composed not only of matter but of energy, a network of vibrational frequencies that interact with the energy of the universe. In these traditions, the mind is seen as the lens through which this energy is perceived and directed, and the body as the vessel through which it flows. Practices such as Reiki, acupuncture, and energy healing aim to balance and align the body's energy system, facilitating the free flow of life force and promoting overall well-being. These practices are rooted in the understanding that physical health is not just a matter of physical anatomy, but of the smooth and harmonious flow of energy throughout the body.

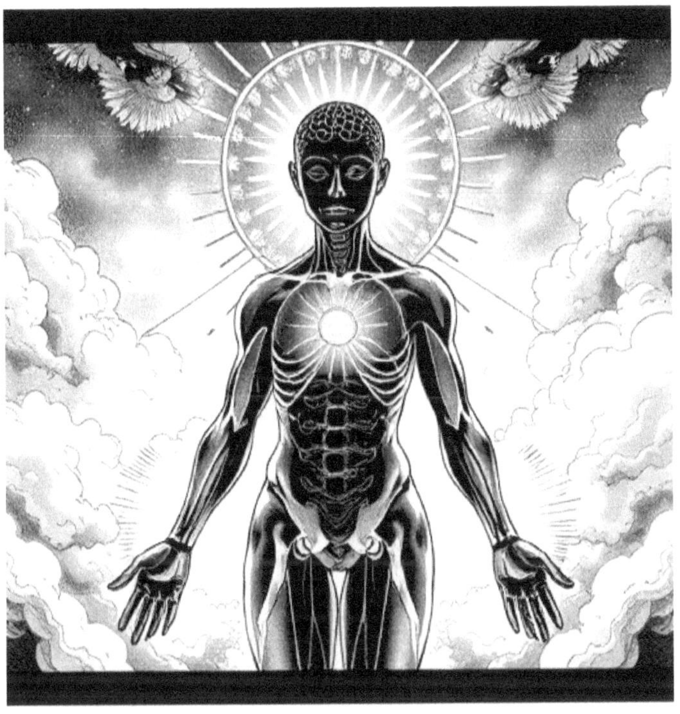

The spiritual dimensions of the mind-body connection suggest that when energy is blocked or out of balance, it can manifest as physical illness or emotional distress. Therefore, healing the body is not simply about addressing symptoms, but about restoring the balance of energy within the system. One of the most powerful ways the mind influences the body is through the practice of conscious awareness, particularly in the form of mindfulness and meditation. These practices, which encourage a non-judgmental awareness of the present moment, have been shown to reduce stress, improve emotional regulation, and enhance overall health. In fact, mindfulness has become a cornerstone of modern therapeutic approaches such as mindfulness-based stress reduction (MBSR) and mindfulness-based cognitive therapy (MBCT), both of which have been shown to be effective in treating conditions such as depression, anxiety, chronic pain, and even PTSD. Through these practices, individuals learn to observe their thoughts and feelings without attachment, allowing them to break free from the cycle of stress, negative thinking, and emotional reactivity that so often leads to physical ailments. This ability to detach from the mind's automatic responses and cultivate a sense of inner peace is not only beneficial for mental health, but also for physical well-being, as it can lower blood pressure, reduce inflammation, and boost immune function.

The mind's ability to influence the body is not limited to emotional and mental states; it also extends to the way we perceive the world around us. Our beliefs, attitudes, and perceptions shape not only our mental and emotional states but also our physical experiences. This is the basis of the concept of somatization, where unresolved emotional conflicts or psychological stress manifest as physical symptoms. For example, someone who is chronically anxious may develop tension in their shoulders or neck, or someone with deep emotional grief may experience digestive issues or headaches. These physical symptoms are not simply the result of physical causes, but are expressions of the mind-body connection, showing us that what happens in the mind can be directly felt in the body. In this way, the mind is not just a passive observer of the body's experiences, but an active participant in shaping the physical body's responses to the world. On the flip side, the body also has a profound influence on the mind. Physical activity, nutrition, and sleep all have significant effects on mental health and emotional regulation. Regular exercise, for instance, has been shown to reduce symptoms of depression and anxiety by releasing endorphins, improving blood flow to the brain, and promoting the growth of new neural connections. Similarly, proper nutrition and adequate sleep are essential for maintaining cognitive function, emotional stability, and physical health. The body, in this sense, is not merely a machine that carries the mind; it is an essential partner in the mind's ability to function optimally. This highlights the importance of cultivating both physical and mental health, as one cannot be truly healthy without the other. Ultimately, the mind-body connection reveals a fundamental truth: that we are not just our thoughts or our bodies, but a dynamic interplay of both. To live a healthy, balanced life, we must attend to both our mental and physical well-being, recognizing that they are inextricably linked and that true health arises from the harmony between mind, body, and spirit. As we cultivate greater awareness of this connection, we are able to heal on deeper levels—physical, emotional, and spiritual—and experience a more integrated, harmonious existence. Bridging the physical and the spiritual is not about transcending the body, but about recognizing that the body itself is sacred, and that the mind, when aligned with the body's wisdom, can guide us to a deeper understanding of our true nature. In this integrated state, we come to realize that the mind and body are not separate, but two aspects of the same unified field of consciousness—an ever-evolving dance of energy, perception, and experience. Through this understanding, we begin to live more consciously, embracing both the physical and spiritual dimensions of our being, and allowing the mind-body connection to guide us toward greater health, peace, and self-realization.

ᚦᚦᚦ

Let us see a short story related to this.

In a kingdom nestled between towering mountains and a fertile river valley, there lived a prince named Ashoka. From the outside, his life seemed perfect. He was strong, handsome, and admired by all who knew him. Yet, despite his outward success and privilege, Ashoka carried a deep, unspoken unease within. He was often plagued by sleepless nights and recurring illnesses, his body growing weak with every passing season. Though he visited the finest physicians in the land, none could explain the source of his suffering.

One day, after yet another night of tossing and turning, Ashoka wandered deep into the forest, seeking solace. As he walked through the trees, his mind heavy with confusion, he came across an old, humble hermit sitting by a quiet stream. The hermit had a calm, peaceful demeanor, and Ashoka felt an immediate pull toward him.

"I am troubled," Ashoka said, sitting beside the hermit. "Though I have all that one could desire—wealth, health, and power—I feel as though my body betrays me. I am often ill, restless, and unhappy. I have sought out many healers, but none have been able to cure me. What is the source of my suffering?"

The hermit looked at him with wise, gentle eyes. "You seek a cure for your body, but what of your mind, young prince? Have you looked within?"

Ashoka, frustrated and weary, sighed. "What do you mean? I am healthy in body. I do not have time for contemplation. I have armies to command, lands to govern."

The hermit smiled softly and spoke in a calm, clear voice, "The body and mind are not separate, Ashoka. They are two parts of the same whole. When one is out of balance, the other suffers. The illness of the body is often the reflection of an illness in the mind. Your body is simply responding to the disquiet in *your heart and thoughts. If you wish to heal, you must first seek peace within."*

The prince stared at him, baffled. "I do not understand. How can my thoughts cause my body to be ill?"

The hermit gestured toward the stream. "The stream flows freely when there are no obstacles in its path, but when rocks and debris are in the way, the water becomes turbulent. So too with your mind. When your thoughts are full of anger, fear, and distraction, they disrupt the flow of your energy. This imbalance creates illness in your body. To heal, you must learn to clear the obstacles in your mind."

Ashoka, still uncertain but intrigued, sat in silence. The hermit continued.

"Sit with me for a while, Ashoka. Let the river teach you. Just as the body and mind are connected, so too is the body and nature. Let go of your struggle. Sit still. Breathe."

Reluctantly, the prince followed the hermit's instructions. He closed his eyes and began to focus on his breath. At first, his mind raced with worries about his kingdom, his duties, his failures. But slowly, he began to notice something strange: the more he let go of his thoughts, the more relaxed his body became. His tense muscles softened. The pressure in his chest began to ease.

As the minutes passed, the air seemed to grow still around him. The wind ceased its movement, the river's murmur quieted, and Ashoka felt as though time itself had paused. A deep, unfamiliar sense of peace settled within him. For the first time in years, his mind was not weighed down by the demands of his life.

When he opened his eyes, the hermit was still sitting beside him, smiling. "Now you begin to understand. The body reflects the mind's turmoil, just as the earth mirrors the heavens. But when the mind becomes calm, the body follows. When you find stillness, you restore balance."

Ashoka's face softened with realization. "I have spent my life chasing after external power, but I see now that the true strength lies within—within the peace of my mind and the harmony of my body. I have been so focused on what I cannot control that I neglected the most important part of my existence."

The hermit nodded. "Indeed. The body is not a machine to be controlled, nor is the mind an enemy to be conquered. They are partners, each dependent on the other for balance and harmony. Your mind shapes your body, just as your body reflects the state

of your mind."

Over the next several days, Ashoka stayed with the hermit, learning the ways of mindfulness, meditation, and physical exercises designed to unify the body and mind. The hermit taught him the ancient practice of yoga, showing him that each posture, each breath, could serve to harmonize the energies within him. He also introduced Ashoka to the art of breathing meditation, where the prince would sit still and observe his thoughts without judgment, letting them pass like clouds in the sky. As he practiced, Ashoka felt a deep shift occur—not just in his body, but in his spirit.

Slowly, the prince's once-constant ailments began to fade. His body grew stronger, his mind clearer. His moods, once erratic and volatile, became steady and calm. And with this newfound harmony came a deeper understanding of himself and his kingdom.

When he returned to his palace, Ashoka ruled with a new sense of balance. He understood now that true leadership came from within, from the stillness and clarity of a peaceful mind, and the wisdom of a body in balance. His people, too, began to notice the change in him, for his newfound tranquility rippled through the court. He treated others with greater compassion and patience, recognizing the mind-body connection in those around him. When ministers or soldiers grew ill or anxious, he would counsel them in the same way the hermit had counseled him—by encouraging them to find balance within themselves, through meditation, mindfulness, and physical well-being.

Years passed, and Ashoka's kingdom flourished, not because of his strength or military might, but because of the peace that emanated from his being. He became a wise ruler, not only because of his intellect but because he understood the interconnectedness of the body, mind, and spirit.

As he grew older, Ashoka visited the hermit once more. The old man was sitting by the same stream, his hair now white as snow. Ashoka approached him, bowing with deep respect.

"You were right, master. I understand now. The mind and body are not separate, but two parts of the same whole. I have found peace, not in my kingdom, but within myself."

The hermit smiled, his eyes twinkling with the wisdom of ages. "You have found the lotus of balance, Ashoka. Just as the lotus blooms in the mud, so too can you find peace amidst the chaos of the world. The mind and body are like two wings of the same bird. When they are in harmony, the bird soars."

Ashoka bowed deeply. "I will carry this wisdom with me always."

And so, the prince turned king, now a true leader, lived the rest of his life in peace—both in body and spirit. The people of his kingdom, too, learned the ways of harmony, and the land became a place where both the body and the mind were cared for equally. Ashoka's legacy was not just in his rule, but in the profound understanding he passed on—**the understanding that the mind and body are not separate entities, but interconnected, and that true health and peace arise when both are in balance.**

FOUR

MEDITATION: THE PATH TO STILLNESS AND AWAKENING

Meditation is not just a practice; it is an unfolding journey, a way of returning to the essence of who we are—an invitation to let go of the incessant chatter of the mind and to enter a state of stillness that allows for deep awareness and transformation. At its heart, meditation is a path to spiritual awakening, a means of reconnecting with the present moment and discovering the profound peace that lies beneath the surface of our thoughts, emotions, and distractions. The origins of meditation are ancient, with roots stretching across millennia, from the contemplative traditions of Buddhism, Hinduism, Taoism, and the mystical practices of Christianity, Islam, and Judaism, to name a few. Across these diverse traditions, meditation has been used as a way to transcend the ego, quiet the mind, and connect to a higher state of consciousness. The underlying principle of all forms of meditation is simple: to cultivate awareness by turning inward, allowing the noise and distractions of the outer world to recede, and focusing on the stillness that lies at the core of being. Despite the variety of forms meditation may take—from mindfulness meditation, transcendental meditation, and loving-kindness meditation, to Zen practices, guided visualization, and body scanning—the essence remains the same: to calm the mind and awaken to the present moment, free from the judgments and distractions of the past and future. At first glance, meditation may seem like a passive activity, an escape from the hustle and bustle of the world, but in reality, it is one of the most powerful tools for personal growth and awakening. When we meditate, we are not merely sitting in silence, waiting for something to happen. We are actively engaging in the process of letting go—letting go of the endless stream of thoughts that normally dominate our consciousness, letting go of our attachments to external events, and letting go of our sense of separation from the world around us. In this sense, meditation is an act of liberation, a conscious effort to transcend the ego's grip on our sense of self and experience the world from a place of pure awareness.

As we quiet the mind and enter into stillness, we begin to uncover a deeper truth: that the true nature of our being is not defined by the endless fluctuations of the mind, but by the unchanging awareness that lies beneath them. This awareness is the essence of who we are, the silent witness that observes the comings and goings of thoughts, feelings, and sensations without attachment or identification. Over time, meditation enables us to access this deeper state of awareness more consistently, cultivating a profound sense of inner peace, clarity, and insight. But meditation is not just a tool for inner peace—it is also a powerful vehicle for spiritual awakening. In many spiritual traditions, the purpose of meditation is to transcend the limitations of the ego and to awaken to a higher state of consciousness. This awakening is not merely an intellectual understanding but a direct, lived experiences—a deep realization that our individual consciousness is not separate from the universal consciousness that pervades all of existence. In this state of awakening, we come to see that the distinctions we create between self and other, subject and object are illusions, and that at the deepest level, all is one. This awakening is the heart of meditation: a profound shift in perception that transforms our relationship with ourselves, others, and the world around us. Meditation thus becomes both a means of personal transformation and a path toward spiritual liberation, allowing us to experience the deeper dimensions of reality and to awaken to our true nature as beings of pure consciousness. But the path to awakening through meditation is not without its challenges. It requires commitment, patience, and discipline, as well as the willingness to face the resistance that inevitably arises when we confront the mind's relentless distractions. In the early stages of meditation, it is common to encounter frustration as the mind constantly pulls us away from the present moment, enticing us with thoughts of the past or future, worries about the future, or judgments about our meditation practice. This is where the real work of meditation begins—learning to sit with discomfort, to observe the mind without judgment, and to gently guide our attention back to the present moment. It is a process of cultivation, where we train ourselves to be more aware, more mindful, and more present. Over time, with consistent practice, the restless energy of the mind begins to settle, and a profound stillness emerges. This stillness is not emptiness, but a deep, vibrant presence that allows us to experience the world with greater clarity, sensitivity, and openness. The mind becomes a tool, rather than a master, and we learn to move through life with a sense of ease and flow. In this way, meditation is not just about quieting the mind, but about transforming our relationship to the mind itself. It is an invitation to step beyond the limitations of our habitual thought patterns, to access the deeper currents of awareness, and to awaken to the vastness of our true nature.

As we continue on this path, we begin to realize that the process of meditation is not something that happens "in here" while we are sitting on a cushion or lying down in stillness. The true gift of meditation lies in how it transforms the way we live our lives. As we deepen our practice, we find that the stillness and clarity cultivated in meditation begin to permeate every aspect of our lives—our interactions with others, our response to challenges, and our sense of connection to the world around us. The peace and awareness we find within become more than just personal experiences; they become a lens through which we see and interact with the world. In this way, meditation teaches us to live more consciously, more authentically, and more compassionately. The insight gained from meditation opens us to new levels of understanding, revealing that we are not isolated individuals, but interconnected expressions of the same universal consciousness. The heart of this realization is awakening—awakening to the truth of who we are, to the depth of our inner being, and to the oneness that exists beyond all apparent separation. This awakening is not a distant goal, but a living reality that we can access in every moment, simply by turning inward and embracing the stillness that resides at the core of our being. Through consistent practice, we come to realize that meditation is not something we do to "achieve" something, but rather a process of returning to our true nature. It is the rediscovery of who we have always been—beings of infinite potential, unbounded by time, space, or circumstance. In this way, meditation is not a technique or a practice in the conventional sense, but an invitation to live from a deeper, more awakened place within. As we walk this path, we are continually reminded that the essence of life is not to be found in the outer world, but in the silent presence that exists within us all. Meditation is the path to that presence, the gateway to awakening, and the key to living a life of profound peace, love, and wisdom.

ϷϷϷ

Let us see a short story related to this.

Once, in an ancient kingdom nestled between the green hills and golden fields, there lived a young man named Mohan. He had spent his life in the bustling city of his ancestors, a city known for its grand markets, busy streets, and the constant hum of activity. The people in the city were always moving, chasing after wealth, recognition, and the pleasures of the world. Mohan, however, often felt a sense of emptiness amidst the noise, a yearning for something deeper than the distractions of daily life.

He had heard from the wise elders that true peace could be found not in the external world but in the quiet of the mind. One day, after a particularly restless night, Mohan decided to seek out a teacher who could guide him toward this peace. He heard of a revered sage who lived in the mountains, far from the distractions of the city, and who was said to have mastered the art of meditation.

Mohan traveled for days, through forests and across rivers, until he reached the sage's humble dwelling—a small, wooden hut by a serene river. The sage, an elderly man with silver hair and a kind face, greeted him warmly and invited him to sit.

"I have come to learn the art of meditation," Mohan said. "I seek peace, stillness, and a way to quiet my restless mind."

The sage nodded gently. "Peace, like a river, flows naturally when it is not obstructed. The mind, much like a turbulent river, is full of distractions, thoughts, and desires that create ripples on the surface. Our task is to quiet the mind, like stilling the water, to see the depths beneath. Would you like to learn this stillness?"

Mohan, eager to learn, nodded eagerly. "Yes, please. Teach me how to quiet my mind."

The sage smiled. "Meditation is not about achieving something, Mohan. It is about letting go of what you think you need. It is about returning to the stillness that is always present within you. Come, sit by the river with me."

The two walked to the riverbank. The water was clear and flowed gently, but Mohan could see the small ripples made by leaves and twigs floating downstream.

"Look at the river," the sage said. "At this moment, the water seems peaceful, but it is full of activity beneath the surface.

Thoughts, like these ripples, constantly disturb our awareness. When we meditate, we try to still these ripples. But just as the water of the river will always return to movement, so too will our thoughts. The key is not to fight them but to observe them without attachment."

Mohan sat down beside the sage, his legs crossed and his hands resting on his knees. The sage instructed him to close his eyes and focus on his breath.

"As you breathe, let your thoughts come and go like the ripples in the river. Don't try to stop them. Simply observe. With time, you will notice that the water beneath the ripples—your true nature—remains still, even if the surface moves."

At first, Mohan found it difficult. His mind raced with thoughts of the city, of his family, and of his ambitions. Each thought felt like a boulder thrown into the river, sending waves of distraction through his mind. But he remembered the sage's words and gently returned his focus to his breath.

Days turned into weeks, and each day, Mohan meditated by the river. Sometimes, he could feel moments of peace when the ripples of his thoughts calmed, and he was able to experience the stillness beneath. But other days, the thoughts seemed overwhelming, and he felt frustrated.

One morning, as he meditated, Mohan became aware of something new. The river, which he had seen countless times, now appeared different. He saw that the ripples on the surface were only temporary, while the deep current beneath flowed with a quiet, unbroken flow. The same current, he realized, was flowing through him. His mind, his emotions, his body—these were all like the ripples on the surface, constantly shifting. But beneath it all, there was an unchanging stillness, an awareness that had always been there.

Suddenly, Mohan understood. The mind, like the river, was not something to be tamed or eliminated; it was simply a reflection of the vastness of his being. The key was not to control the mind, but to observe it, to allow it to flow naturally, without becoming attached to any particular thought or emotion. In that moment, he experienced what the sages had described as satori, a sudden awakening—a deep realization that his true self was not his thoughts or desires, but the awareness that observed them.

When he opened his eyes, he saw the sage watching him with a gentle smile.

"Do you see now?" the sage asked.

Mohan nodded, his heart full of peace. "Yes. The river is not separate from me. It is me."

The sage chuckled softly. "Indeed. And so are you. The river, the trees, the sky, the mountains, and even the clouds—they are all expressions of the same awareness, the same stillness. In meditation, we learn to realize this interconnectedness, to awaken to the truth of our own nature. This is the essence of peace."

Mohan spent many more days meditating by the river. With time, the mind became less of a distraction, and the stillness within him grew stronger. He realized that meditation was not about achieving a state of perfect peace—it was about returning to the peace that was already within him. Each breath, each moment of awareness, was a step closer to the truth that had always been there, waiting to be discovered.

As he prepared to return to the city, the sage gave him one last piece of wisdom.

"You may return to the world, Mohan," the sage said. "But remember that the river of peace is always flowing within you. You need not escape the world to find it. It is in the very fabric of your life. When you are caught in the currents of distraction, return to your breath, return to the stillness within, and remember that all things arise from the same source."

Mohan thanked the sage, and with a heart full of peace, he returned to the city. Though the noise and busyness of life surrounded him, he found that he could carry the stillness of the river within. The practice of meditation had transformed him, not by changing the world around him, but by changing the way he saw and experienced the world. The restlessness of the mind no longer had the power to pull him into chaos. Instead, he had learned to observe the ripples and return to the deep current of peace beneath.

And so, as the days passed, Mohan moved through life not with the constant turbulence of distraction, but with the quiet wisdom of the silent river, remembering always that the **peace he sought was never outside of him—it was always flowing within.**

FIVE

THE UNIVERSAL ONENESS: CONNECTING WITH THE DIVINE

The concept of Universal Oneness is as old as human consciousness itself, appearing in sacred texts, mystical traditions, and philosophical musings from every culture across time. Whether expressed as the realization of an ultimate reality, an interconnected divine fabric of existence, or an essential unity beneath the surface of apparent duality, the idea that everything is interconnected and that all beings arise from a single source is one of the most profound and universally shared truths in human history. It points to a reality in which separation is but an illusion, and the essence of the Divine pervades everything, from the smallest particle to the vast cosmos. In this understanding, there is no 'other,' no division between the sacred and the mundane, no separation between the self and the rest of the world. Oneness is not merely a metaphysical abstraction but an experiential reality that can be accessed through deep inner awareness, spiritual practice, and a shift in consciousness. For many, the path toward experiencing this unity involves transcending the ego—the false sense of self that is constructed by thoughts, desires, and external identifications—and coming into direct contact with the essence of the self, which is not isolated or separate but an integral part of the whole. This process of awakening to oneness is at the heart of nearly all spiritual practices, whether through meditation, prayer, contemplation, or acts of selfless love. In the yogic tradition, for instance, the pursuit of oneness is articulated through the concept of Advaita (non-duality), which teaches that the individual soul (Atman) is ultimately the same as the universal soul (Brahman).

In this view, the apparent multiplicity of forms, lives, and objects is simply the expression of a single, undivided reality, and the true goal of human life is to recognize this oneness through self-inquiry and spiritual discipline. Similarly, in the mystical traditions of Christianity, the Sufism of Islam, and the teachings of Buddhism, the idea of connecting with the divine is not about creating a relationship with a distant God, but recognizing that the Divine is inherent within us and all around us. The world itself, in all its diversity, is seen as an expression of the One, and the task of the seeker is to awaken to the interconnectedness of all things. In mystical Christianity, for example, the writings of saints like John of the Cross and Meister Eckhart speak of a deep union with the Divine, a state where the self and God are no longer seen as separate but as one. This union, however, is not a mental or intellectual understanding, but a direct, lived experience of communion with the Divine presence that transcends the boundaries of the self. In this mystical union, the seeker comes to realize that they are not separate from God or the world, but are an integral expression of the Divine, a wave in the vast ocean of universal consciousness. The concept of Oneness is also reflected in the teachings of quantum physics, which reveal that at the most fundamental level, all matter is interconnected. Subatomic particles do not exist in isolation but are part of a vast web of energy and information that transcends space and time. This discovery, while grounded in empirical science, echoes the ancient spiritual understanding that all things arise from a single, unified source. The interconnectedness of all things is not just a spiritual metaphor, but a truth that can be observed and verified through the lens of modern science. However, the full depth of this unity is something that cannot be fully grasped by the intellect alone—it must be directly experienced. And this is where the role of spiritual practice becomes essential. Meditation, prayer, mindfulness, and acts of service are all pathways to this experience of oneness, as they help quiet the mind, dissolve the barriers of the ego, and allow the individual to feel their connection to the greater whole. The stillness and silence of meditation, for example, provide a space in which the individual can move beyond the limiting perceptions of the self, and touch the deeper, infinite aspects of consciousness that transcend individuality. In this state, the practitioner may experience a sense of unity with the cosmos, a direct experience of divine presence, or a profound feeling of interconnectedness with all beings. This is not merely a temporary state of peace or bliss, but a permanent shift in perception—a realization that one's true nature is not separate, isolated, or defined by the body or mind, but is part of the vast, undivided web of life. Yet, the experience of oneness is not solely about transcending the self, but also about deepening one's relationship with the world in its multiplicity.

Recognizing the interconnectedness of all things does not mean denying the uniqueness of individual experiences or the diversity of life forms, but rather embracing them in the context of a larger, unified whole. This realization transforms the way we relate to others, to the earth, and to the Divine. It fosters compassion, empathy, and love, as we come to understand that every living being, every tree, every animal, every person, is a unique expression of the same underlying truth. This insight into oneness also calls forth a deep sense of responsibility. If all is interconnected, then every thought, word, and action has the potential to affect the whole. Spiritual awakening, therefore, is not just about personal liberation but about taking responsibility for one's impact on the world. The awakened individual understands that their actions ripple through the web of life, affecting not only themselves but all of creation. Thus, the recognition of oneness is intrinsically linked to the ethical imperative of living in harmony with all beings and with the earth itself. It calls us to act with wisdom, kindness, and humility, and to live with an awareness of our connection to the greater web of life. The path of oneness is also a journey toward love—unconditional, boundless love that recognizes no boundaries, no distinctions between self and other. It is the love that flows naturally when we realize that we are not separate from those around us, that every living being shares the same divine spark. This love is not contingent on personal gain or approval, but flows freely from the recognition of shared existence. It is a love that transcends attachment and is grounded in the understanding that at the deepest level, all beings are manifestations of the Divine.

Connecting with the Divine, then, is not about reaching toward something beyond us, but about recognizing the Divine within and all around us. The Divine is not confined to religious dogma or external rituals but is immanent in every moment, every breath, and every encounter. The more we awaken to this presence, the more we realize that the Divine is not a distant God to be worshipped, but an intimate presence to be experienced, embodied, and lived. This experience of the Divine is not reserved for mystics or saints; it is available to all who are willing to open their hearts and minds to the truth of oneness. In this understanding, the search for God or the Divine is not about seeking something separate, but about recognizing the inherent divinity of all creation, and awakening to our own divine nature. As we deepen our experience of oneness, we come to realize that the Divine is not an abstract concept or a distant deity but the very fabric of existence itself. To connect with the Divine is to recognize that we are the Divine, that we are expressions of an infinite consciousness that is both immanent and transcendent. And in this realization, we find true liberation—not from the world, but in the world, as we recognize the sacredness of all things and live in harmony with the underlying unity of existence.

ᐅᐅᐅ

Let us see a short story related to this.

In a distant kingdom, nestled between lush green mountains and flowing rivers, there was a sacred temple known as the Temple of the Golden Lotus. The temple, though small, was revered by all for its deep spiritual significance. It was said that within its walls lay an ancient statue of a lotus flower, made entirely of gold, that was the embodiment of the universe itself. The temple's priests and seekers from all over the land came to meditate before it, hoping to glimpse the divine essence it represented.

One such seeker was a young woman named Lila, who had lived her entire life in the bustling city near the temple. She had heard stories of the Golden Lotus and its power to reveal the deepest truths of existence. Lila was not like the other seekers who came to the temple with religious devotion or philosophical knowledge; instead, she sought to understand the great mystery of life, the source of all things, and her place within it.

Lila had spent many years studying the teachings of sages, mystics, and philosophers. From the ancient wisdom of India to the writings of Greek philosophers, she had learned of the concept of Universal Oneness—the idea that all things are interconnected and that every being arises from a single source. She had studied Advaita (non-duality) in the Yogic tradition, learned of the mystical unity in Christianity, and even read the teachings of Sufism. Despite her intellectual understanding, something was missing—she could not grasp the experience of oneness, the lived reality of it.

So, Lila traveled to the temple with the hope that by meditating before the Golden Lotus, she would finally touch the essence of what she had only understood with her mind.

On the first day of her arrival, Lila entered the temple with reverence. The air was thick with the scent of incense, and the golden statue of the lotus gleamed softly in the light of the setting sun. It was more magnificent than she had ever imagined. She sat before it in silence, attempting to quiet her mind and surrender to the stillness. Hours passed, but her mind remained restless. Thoughts of the world outside, of her family, her studies, and her doubts, kept intruding. She felt frustrated, as if she were missing something essential.

On the second day, Lila returned again, this time determined to empty herself of all preconceived ideas and expectations. She closed her eyes and breathed deeply, allowing the quietness of the temple to settle into her being. Yet, even as she calmed her mind, she still felt a deep sense of separation. She felt like an individual, a separate entity trying to connect with something beyond her reach.

As Lila meditated, she became aware of a soft voice that seemed to arise from the depths of her being, not as words but as a kind of knowing. She opened her eyes and turned around. There, standing at the entrance of the temple, was an elderly monk, his face serene and wise, with eyes that seemed to hold the entire sky within them.

"Are you searching for the Lotus of Oneness?" the monk asked, his voice gentle but clear.

Lila nodded, though she could not find words to explain her struggle.

The monk smiled and stepped closer. "You seek to understand, but the understanding you seek is not something to be grasped by the mind. It is not a concept to be learned. It is the reality beneath your thoughts, the truth of the space in which all things arise."

Lila looked confused. "But I have studied the sacred texts. I understand the teachings of Advaita, of the unity of all things. Why can't I experience it?"

The monk sat beside her and gestured to the Golden Lotus. "Look at this flower. It is beautiful, isn't it?"

Lila nodded, her gaze drawn to the golden petals that shimmered in the temple light.

"This flower," the monk continued, "appears separate, does it not? But in truth, it is not separate from the earth, the sunlight, the water, or the air. It is made of the same elements that make up the rivers, the mountains, and the clouds. It is no different from the soil beneath your feet or the wind above your head. All things are interconnected in the web of life, arising from the same source."

Lila was quiet, pondering the monk's words. "But how do I experience this oneness? How do I feel connected to the world like this flower is?"

The monk smiled again. "You do not need to do anything. You do not need to reach out to feel the oneness; it is already here, within you and all around you. The challenge is not to become one with the world, but to realize that you are the world. The boundaries you see between yourself and the rest of creation are illusory. In truth, there is no 'other.' There is only one continuous flow of energy, and you are a wave in that flow."

Lila looked at the monk, her heart opening with a sense of recognition. But the next moment, doubt crept in again. "But if we are all one, why does suffering exist? Why is there so much pain in the world?"

The monk's expression softened. "The world is filled with suffering because it is filled with separation—the illusion of separation. People see themselves as separate from others, from nature, from the Divine. But when you understand the truth of Oneness, you will see that the suffering of others is your suffering, the pain of the earth is your pain. And through this recognition, compassion arises naturally. You cannot separate yourself from the world without causing harm to the whole. But when you know that you are one with all, you live with kindness, with wisdom, with love."

Lila sat in silence, the monk's words resonating deeply within her. For the first time in her life, she felt a stirring of truth, a subtle but profound shift in her consciousness. It was not an intellectual understanding, but an inner knowing that arose from beyond the mind.

As she sat before the Golden Lotus, Lila felt a deep sense of connection to everything—her breath, the temple walls, the trees outside, the birds in the sky, the mountains in the distance. It was as if she had always been a part of it all, and the illusion of separation had dissolved. In that moment, she understood that the lotus was not something separate from her, but a reflection of the same divine energy that moved through all beings. The essence of the Lotus, the essence of Oneness, was the same essence that flowed through her.

The monk rose to leave, but before he did, he turned to Lila and said, "Now that you have seen, you must live what you have realized. The path of Oneness is not found in seeking, but in living. Let your actions, your thoughts, your love, reflect the truth you now carry within."

With that, the monk disappeared into the temple's shadows, leaving Lila alone with the Golden Lotus. And for the first time, she felt at peace. She realized that the search for oneness was not a journey of the mind, but of the heart—**a journey of remembrance, not discovery.**

SIX

THE ROLE OF INTUITION IN SPIRITUALITY

Intuition, often described as a "knowing without knowing," is one of the most profound yet enigmatic aspects of human consciousness. While reason and logic dominate much of our everyday decision-making, intuition offers an alternative—an inner knowing that bypasses the linear thinking of the mind, often arriving spontaneously and unbidden. In the spiritual context, intuition is more than just a mental shortcut; it is considered a bridge to higher consciousness, a way to connect with deeper wisdom and divine guidance. Historically, intuition has been valued across a wide range of spiritual traditions and mystical practices. In ancient cultures, intuition was often revered as a sacred faculty that connected individuals to the divine, the unseen realms, and higher states of being. In Greek philosophy, for instance, the concept of *nous* (intuitive intellect) was considered the highest form of knowing, transcending the limitations of ordinary, discursive thought. Similarly, in Hinduism, the practice of *dhyana* (meditation) is believed to open the mind to intuitive perception, leading one to realize the ultimate truth of *Brahman* (the absolute reality).

In Western mysticism, intuitive insights are often seen as glimpses into the divine, revelations that are not comprehended by the mind, but are felt deeply in the heart and spirit. Despite its universal presence across cultures and religions, intuition is often misunderstood, especially in modern, rational societies. Today, intuition is frequently dismissed as irrational or even illogical, something to be skeptical of in a world that values empirical evidence and reason. Yet, spiritual traditions throughout history tell a different story, presenting intuition as a form of inner wisdom that connects us to the divine source of all creation. Intuition, in this sense, is a way to receive guidance from the higher realms, whether from the soul, the divine, or the collective unconscious. The intuitive process is not bound by time or space, often providing insights into situations or truths that the intellect cannot fathom. It is, in essence, the language of the soul—a way of perceiving that transcends ordinary human cognition and connects the individual to the larger universal consciousness.

Intuition is also considered a vital tool in spiritual growth. On the path of self-realization, one learns to trust and cultivate this inner knowing, using it as a compass to navigate the complexities of life. The spiritual seeker, through meditation, contemplation, and self-inquiry, refines their ability to discern between the voice of the ego (which often masquerades as intuition) and the true, higher guidance that arises from the soul. This discernment is crucial, as intuition can sometimes be clouded by personal desires, fears, or attachments, which distort the clarity of the guidance. However, when properly honed, intuition becomes an infallible source of direction and insight, guiding the practitioner towards deeper spiritual truths and alignment with the divine will. The cultivation of intuition, therefore, is central to spiritual development. It involves not just passive receptivity but active engagement with the inner life, cultivating silence, inner stillness, and openness to the flow of wisdom. Spiritual practices such as meditation, prayer, and mindfulness are all designed to quiet the noise of the external world and the incessant chatter of the mind, creating the space in which intuition can arise naturally and clearly. In the Buddhist tradition, for example, meditation is practiced to quiet the mind and open the heart, allowing intuitive insight to emerge from a state of pure awareness. Similarly, in the Christian mystical tradition, contemplative prayer is used to attune the heart and mind to the presence of God, where the voice of the Divine is often heard through a deep, inner knowing. In addition to this, intuition plays a profound role in the experience of *direct knowing* or *gnosis*—a type of spiritual knowledge that arises not from external teachings or intellectual understanding, but from an internal, experiential knowing of truth. This kind of knowing is often described as being more immediate, more intimate, and more profound than conceptual knowledge. It is through intuition that we can experience the Divine directly, without the filter of language, thought, or form. In the moment of gnosis, there is no separation between the knower and the known; intuition leads to a deep realization of oneness with the Divine and with all of creation. Beyond spiritual insight, intuition also facilitates the flow of grace in one's life. When one is in touch with their intuitive guidance, they become more aligned with the natural flow of life, effortlessly receiving answers to their questions, clarity on their path, and the energy to manifest their intentions. Intuition, in this sense, becomes a channel through which the Divine flows into the individual, guiding them not only on their spiritual journey but also in their day-to-day lives. The intuition of the heart aligns with divine wisdom and is the inner compass that leads one to live authentically, in harmony with their true self and their soul's purpose. This alignment is not about intellectual understanding but about attuning to the deeper currents of truth that exist beyond the mind's limited scope. Intuition also plays a crucial role in the development of compassion and empathy. As one becomes more in touch with their inner knowing, they begin to recognize the interconnectedness of all beings. Intuitive perception allows one to feel the emotions, struggles, and joys of others, creating a profound sense of unity and compassion. This is especially important in the practice of loving-kindness (metta) in Buddhism, where intuition helps one to understand the suffering of others and respond with genuine care and compassion. In this way, intuition is not just a tool for personal enlightenment but also a means of deepening one's connection with the world and contributing to the collective healing of humanity. In a practical sense, intuition can be understood as the inner sense that guides us through life, whether in the form of gut feelings, flashes of insight, or spontaneous knowing. It often arises when we need it most, providing us with answers to questions or solutions to problems that seem impossible to solve through ordinary reasoning. People often report having intuitive insights during moments of deep relaxation or altered states of consciousness, where the mind is quiet and receptive. Intuition is also frequently accessed during creative processes, when individuals tap into the wellspring of inspiration and insight that lies beyond the confines of ordinary thought.

As such, intuition is not only a spiritual tool but also a practical one, aiding us in navigating the complexities of life with greater clarity, insight, and purpose. The practice of trusting and following intuition also strengthens one's connection to the divine, as it requires surrendering the need for control and allowing oneself to be guided by a higher wisdom. The more one learns to trust their intuition, the more they begin to see it as a direct communication with the Divine—a subtle whisper of guidance, an inner knowing that leads them toward their highest good. It is through the cultivation of intuition that the spiritual seeker learns to step out of the realm of intellectual understanding and into the realm of direct experience, where the divine presence is felt intimately, personally, and profoundly. To trust intuition is to trust the wisdom of the soul, and in this trust, one finds peace, direction, and alignment with their true purpose in life. Intuition, in its highest form, is the voice of the Divine within, guiding us toward greater wisdom, love, and understanding. The role of intuition in spirituality is not just that of a tool or a practice; it is the key to unlocking the deeper mysteries of life, leading to an embodied experience of the Divine and a profound sense of connection with all of existence. It is through intuition that we come to realize that we are not separate from the Divine but are intimately connected to it, and that all the wisdom, love, and guidance we seek is already present within us, waiting to be accessed through the cultivation of deep inner awareness and trust.

ᛈᛈᛈ

Let us see a short story related to this.

Once upon a time, in a village nestled between the mountains and the sea, there lived a humble weaver named Lira. Known for her exquisite tapestries, Lira's work was revered far and wide. She wove patterns so intricate that it seemed as if her threads were alive, dancing with the light of the moon and shimmering with the warmth of the sun. People marveled at her craftsmanship, but what truly set Lira apart was a gift she had long kept secret: her ability to weave not only with her hands but with her heart, guided by an unseen thread of knowing that led her to create with an almost divine intuition.

Though Lira's tapestries were beautiful, they were not merely decorative; they were filled with hidden messages, divine symbols, and prophetic visions. Each tapestry told a story that transcended time, often showing glimpses of future events, moments of healing, or wisdom that others had yet to uncover. But Lira never spoke of her gift. To the village, she was simply a skilled weaver, but to those who truly listened, her work carried the language of the soul.

One day, a young traveler named Kael arrived at the village. He was a seeker, restless and uncertain of his path. Kael had journeyed through many lands in search of wisdom, but the more he searched, the more lost he felt. He had been trained in the ways of logic and reason, but the deeper mysteries of life—those that could not be understood through study—eluded him.

When Kael entered the village, he was drawn to Lira's humble shop. The tapestries hanging on the walls seemed to call to him, as if they were waiting to speak to him. He approached Lira and asked, "What do your tapestries mean? Why do they seem to speak to me?"

Lira smiled gently and replied, "The threads I weave are not just of silk and wool; they are of intuition, of dreams, of silent knowing. If you wish to understand, you must look beyond the fabric and listen with your heart."

Kael was intrigued but puzzled. "How can I listen with my heart when all I have known is the logic of the mind?" he asked.

Lira's eyes sparkled with understanding. "The mind is like a river—ever flowing, ever thinking. But the heart is like the still lake at the mountain's base, reflecting the heavens above. It is in stillness that the deeper truths are revealed. You must learn to listen with your heart if you seek the wisdom that lies beyond reason."

Over the next several days, Kael stayed in the village, returning each day to Lira's shop, where he would sit quietly, gazing at the tapestries, trying to understand the messages woven within them. He felt a pull, a quiet whisper deep within, *but he could not quite grasp it.*

One evening, after a long day of wandering through the village, Kael returned to the shop and sat before one of Lira's newest tapestries. It depicted a vast ocean, the waves rising and falling like the breath of the earth, with a single ship sailing on its surface. As Kael gazed at it, something stirred within him. His breath slowed, and a deep sense of peace settled in his chest. Suddenly, without knowing how or why, he understood the tapestry. The ship represented his life, adrift upon the waves of uncertainty, but the ocean—the vast, eternal ocean—was the intuitive wisdom of the world, guiding the ship, even when it seemed to be lost.

The realization was both profound and simple. He was not alone. The currents of life, like the ocean, were always moving, always guiding him, even when he could not see them. His journey was part of something greater, a divine flow that would carry him where he needed to go.

Kael turned to Lira, whose eyes were filled with a knowing smile. "How did you know?" he whispered. "How did you create this tapestry?"

Lira placed a gentle hand on his shoulder. "I do not create these tapestries with my mind alone," she said. "I listen. I listen to the world around me, to the wind in the trees, the rhythm of the tides, the song of the birds. And I listen to something deeper—the voice of the soul, the intuitive wisdom that lies within every one of us. It is not a knowing of the mind, but a knowing that is felt, that rises like the dawn, without explanation, without reason."

Kael's heart swelled with understanding, and for the first time in his life, he felt a deep sense of peace. "I have been searching with my mind," he said softly. "But the answers I seek are not in the books or the teachings. They are within me, in the quiet places where my heart can hear."

Lira nodded. "The path to wisdom is not always clear, for the mind loves to seek answers, to label and define. But the heart, when it is still and open, can hear the song of the universe, and in that song, all things are known. Intuition is not a gift given to a few; it is the divine language of the soul, available to all who are willing to listen."

The next morning, as Kael prepared to leave the village, he stopped by Lira's shop one last time. He gazed once more at the tapestry with the ship sailing on the ocean, and this time, he did not merely look. He listened. And in that silence, a voice, soft and gentle, rose from within. **Follow the currents of your heart,**

and you will find your way."

With this, Kael understood. The journey ahead would not be one of logical steps or intellectual pursuits. It would be a journey of listening—to the whispers of his heart, to the subtle guidance of his intuition, and to the divine rhythm of the universe. With a deep breath, he set forth, no longer lost but trusting in the unseen currents that would carry him to where he was meant to be.

SEVEN

HEALING THE SOUL: ENERGY, VIBRATION, AND TRANSFORMATION

The process of healing the soul is a deeply transformative journey, one that requires us to understand that the very essence of our being is not just physical or mental, but fundamentally energetic. At the core of this understanding is the recognition that everything in the universe, including ourselves, is composed of energy, and that energy exists in a state of constant vibration. This view of the human being as a network of energetic frequencies is not a new one—it has been present in various ancient healing systems, such as Traditional Chinese Medicine (TCM), Ayurveda, and indigenous traditions around the world. In these systems, the idea of Qi, Prana, or life force is central to health, suggesting that when this energy flows freely and harmoniously, we experience balance and vitality. However, when the flow of energy becomes blocked, distorted, or stagnant, emotional, mental, or physical ailments manifest. The soul, seen as the deepest layer of our being, is not separate from this energetic field; it is a conduit for universal energy that connects us to the cosmic flow of the universe.

Spiritual practices such as meditation, prayer, sound healing, and energy therapies like Reiki, acupuncture, and crystal healing, work by realigning the energetic frequencies of the individual, restoring harmony to their body, mind, and soul. This energetic approach to healing is underpinned by the idea that all life is interconnected through a web of energy, and that true healing involves not just treating symptoms but addressing the energetic imbalances that lie at the root of illness and suffering. At a scientific level, we can understand energy and vibration through the principles of quantum physics, which reveal that the universe is fundamentally made of energy vibrating at different frequencies. Subatomic particles are not solid matter, but rather energetic waveforms that interact with one another, creating the reality we experience. This understanding challenges the conventional view of the universe as a collection of separate, inert objects and instead presents a reality in which all things are interconnected through an intricate web of energy. The human body, as an energetic system, vibrates at its own frequency, and when this frequency is aligned with the higher frequencies of love, joy, peace, and compassion, the soul experiences healing. In contrast, when the frequency is in dissonance, whether due to unresolved trauma, negative emotions, or limiting beliefs, the soul experiences fragmentation and suffering. Healing the soul, therefore, is about restoring the energetic harmony within the individual, allowing the soul to express itself in its full potential. Vibrational healing practices, such as sound therapy (using the frequencies of singing bowls, tuning forks, or the human voice), work by tuning the body's energetic field to resonate with higher, healing frequencies. These frequencies carry a transformative power that can dissolve energetic blockages and recalibrate the body, mind, and spirit to a state of balance. Similarly, practices like the use of crystals, essential oils, and color therapy are based on the principle that everything vibrates at a unique frequency, and by introducing specific frequencies into the system, we can bring about alignment and healing. The soul, as the eternal essence of our being, is deeply affected by the vibrations we encounter in the world. From the frequencies of music to the vibrations of human emotions, every interaction we have impacts our energy field and contributes to the health or dis-ease of the soul. On a spiritual level, healing the soul involves aligning oneself with the highest possible frequencies—those of love, gratitude, and unity—recognizing that we are all expressions of a single, divine energy. This alignment can occur through various spiritual practices, such as deep contemplation, mindfulness, breathwork, or acts of kindness and service, all of which raise our energetic vibration and create a field of healing both within and around us. When the soul is in a state of alignment with its highest vibrational frequency, it experiences a profound sense of peace, purpose, and connection with the divine.

The transformative power of soul healing is not limited to the individual but extends to the collective. As each person raises their vibrational frequency through healing practices, they contribute to the larger field of collective consciousness, uplifting the global energy and creating a ripple effect of positive change. This process of personal and collective transformation is essential in the healing of humanity and the planet. The idea that the universe is energy and vibration not only holds spiritual significance but also brings a new perspective on how we approach personal healing and global healing. It invites us to move beyond the materialistic and mechanistic worldview, which separates us from the interconnectedness of life, and to embrace a holistic, energetic understanding of health and wellbeing. When we begin to perceive ourselves as vibrational beings in harmony with the universe, we unlock our own healing potential and become active participants in the larger process of universal transformation. On a deeper level, healing the soul is also about reconnecting with the divine source of all creation. The soul, in its highest state, is a reflection of divine consciousness, an expression of pure energy that transcends time, space, and form. The journey of soul healing is, therefore, a journey of return—a return to the source from which we came, to the divine vibration that is the foundation of all existence. Through practices that align us with divine energy, such as prayer, devotion, or immersion in nature, we can open ourselves to the infinite well of healing that resides within us. This sacred connection to the divine is the ultimate source of healing, as it restores the soul to its original state of purity, wholeness, and love. In this way, healing the soul is not merely about fixing what is broken, but about rediscovering our true nature—our inherent connection to the divine energy that flows through all things. As we heal, we return to a state of unity, where the boundaries between the self and the universe dissolve, and we experience the divine presence in all aspects of life. The soul's healing is thus a continual process of raising our vibration, aligning with divine energy, and embodying our highest potential. This on-going transformation leads to profound spiritual growth, a deep sense of inner peace, and a conscious connection to the universal flow of energy that binds all of existence together. Ultimately, healing the soul is about awakening to the truth of who we are, realizing that we are not separate from the divine, but are expressions of the same eternal energy that flows through the entire universe. Through energy, vibration, and transformation, we come into alignment with the divine blueprint of creation, experiencing a life of wholeness, harmony, and spiritual fulfilment.

ϷϷϷ

Let us see a short story related to this.

In the heart of an ancient forest, where the trees whispered the secrets of the universe and the winds carried the echoes of forgotten wisdom, there was a village where healing was not only a practice but a way of life. The villagers knew that true healing went beyond the body and mind; it was the soul that needed mending when the storms of life left their mark. They called it the "Song of the Soul"—the idea that each being vibrated with a unique frequency, and when this song was in harmony with the universe, peace, and joy flowed through them like a river. But when the song was out of tune, there was pain, suffering, and dissonance.

Among these villagers was a wise woman named Kalina, known for her ability to heal not just the body, but the very soul of those who came to her. She was a guardian of ancient knowledge passed down from her ancestors—the people of the hills and the rivers, the practitioners of sacred arts who had long known the truth that all life was connected by the threads of energy, and that healing the soul was a process of realigning one's inner vibration with the cosmic harmony. Kalina's methods were unconventional: she would use sounds, crystals, and symbols, and even the natural vibrations of the forest itself to help those in need.

One day, a young man named Eron arrived in the village. His face was pale, his eyes dull, and his movements sluggish *as though he were carrying an invisible weight. He had heard of Kalina's wisdom from travelers passing through the village and had come in search of healing, though he did not fully understand what it was that he needed.*

Kalina greeted him with kindness and a knowing smile. "Eron, you are burdened," she said, sensing the discord in his energetic field. "Tell me, what weighs on your heart?"

Eron sighed deeply, his chest tight with the grief of many years. "I have lost my way," he confessed. "I have sought meaning in the wrong places, pursued wealth, power, and fleeting pleasures, but none of it has brought me peace. My heart is heavy, my mind restless, and I feel as if I have become lost to myself. I no longer know who I am."

Kalina nodded, for she had seen many souls like Eron's. "The song of your soul has become out of tune," she said softly. "When we do not live in alignment with our true essence, when we chase after what is fleeting or not our own, our energy becomes fragmented. This creates discord within the body, mind, and spirit, leading to suffering."

"But how can I fix this?" Eron asked, desperate for an answer. "How can I find my way back to harmony?"

Kalina stood and motioned for Eron to follow her into the heart of the forest. The air was thick with the scent of pine and moss, and the rustling of the trees felt like the soft murmur of an ancient prayer. They reached a clearing where a large crystal sat on a stone pedestal, glowing faintly in the dappled sunlight. The crystal was said to contain the wisdom of the earth, and those who were open to its frequency could tap into the greater cosmic song.

Kalina invited Eron to sit before the crystal and close his eyes. "Listen," she instructed. "Let the vibrations of the earth and the air reach you. Feel the energy that flows through all things.

The sound of the wind, the hum of the crystal, the pulse of your own heart—all of these are part of the same song."

At first, Eron felt nothing but silence. His mind was still racing, consumed with worry and doubt. But Kalina's voice, gentle and steady, continued to guide him.

"Release the past," she said. "Let go of all the fears and regrets that bind you to what is no longer real. Feel the vibration of the earth beneath you, steady and unwavering. Feel the breath of the trees, their energy connecting you to all that is."

Slowly, Eron began to feel a faint pulse, like a rhythmic thumping deep within his chest. It was subtle at first, but then, as he focused, it grew stronger. He became aware of the stillness in the forest, the way the air seemed to vibrate with unseen energy. He felt the interconnectedness of all things—the trees, the stones, the animals, and even the stars far above. The harmony of the natural world, which had always been there, began to sink into his bones.

Kalina continued, "The body and the soul are one—when the body's energy is in harmony, so too is the soul's. But when the soul is fragmented, when we forget our true nature, the body feels it. Healing begins when we reconnect with the pure frequency of love, compassion, and truth that is within us all."

Eron closed his eyes and breathed deeply, letting go of the weight that had burdened him for so long. He focused on the vibrations around him, imagining them flowing through him, cleansing him, aligning him with the natural flow of life. He felt a surge of warmth in his heart, a lightness in his chest, and for the first time in years, he experienced a sense of peace—a sense of belonging to something greater than himself.

Kalina watched in silence, knowing that the healing process had begun. "Healing is not about fixing something broken," she explained. "It is about restoring harmony—realigning the soul with its true essence. When we live in tune with the vibration of love, gratitude, and compassion, we raise our own energy to match the higher frequencies of the universe. And when that happens, we are healed, not just as individuals, but as part of the greater whole."

Eron opened his eyes, tears welling up as he finally understood. "I have been searching in the wrong places," he whispered. "I was seeking outside of myself, when the answer was within me all along."

Kalina nodded. "The song of the soul is always there, waiting to be heard. But it is only when we quiet the noise of the world and listen deeply that we can hear its true melody.

And when we do, healing flows through us like a river, sweeping away the debris of fear and pain."

Eron spent many days with Kalina, learning how to align his energy, to meditate, and to reconnect with the natural vibrations of the earth. He learned that healing the soul was not a one-time event, but a continual process of tuning in to the frequencies of love, peace, and connection. He practiced using sound healing, crystals, and breathwork to maintain the harmony of his energy, and gradually, his life began to transform.

As Eron's soul healed, so did his life. He found peace, purpose, and a deep connection to the universe. The people in his village noticed the change in him, and they too began to seek Kalina's guidance. Word spread that healing the soul was a journey of restoring balance, of tuning in to the divine melody that vibrated through all things.

And thus, the village flourished—**not because of wealth or power, but because its people understood that healing begins from within**. They had learned that the soul, like the earth, is a living, breathing force—always in motion, always vibrating, and always seeking to return to its natural, harmonious state.

EIGHT

Life After Life: Reincarnation, Karma, and the Eternal Self

The question of life after death has fascinated humanity for millennia, with various cultures, philosophies, and spiritual traditions offering their own answers to the mystery of what happens to the soul once it leaves the body. In many of these traditions, the idea of reincarnation stands as a central concept—namely, that the soul is eternal and undergoes a cycle of birth, death, and rebirth. Reincarnation is not merely a matter of the soul returning to a physical body but is seen as a journey of spiritual evolution, where each life serves as an opportunity for growth, learning, and the resolution of past karmic patterns. This cyclical view of life and death can be traced back to ancient civilizations such as the Egyptians and the Greeks, but it is most prominently featured in the spiritual philosophies of Hinduism, Buddhism, and various other Eastern traditions. In these belief systems, the soul is understood to be part of a larger cosmic consciousness, and reincarnation is a mechanism by which the soul undergoes the process of purification and self-realization. Through the multiple lifetimes, the soul learns lessons, works through unresolved desires or attachments, and gradually moves closer to liberation or moksha—the state of being freed from the cycle of birth and death. The law of karma, a key aspect of reincarnation, is deeply interwoven with this process. Karma is often understood as the law of cause and effect: the actions, thoughts, and intentions we generate in one life create a karmic imprint that influences our future experiences, both in this life and in future incarnations.

Karma is not seen as a system of judgment or punishment, but rather as a natural law that governs the flow of energy in the universe. It reflects the balance of positive and negative actions, where good deeds, intentions, and thoughts create beneficial outcomes, and harmful actions create suffering or obstacles. This law of cause and effect, however, is not limited to the physical realm but extends to the mental, emotional, and spiritual dimensions of existence. Each lifetime, therefore, is seen as a new opportunity to clear past karmic debts, learn from the mistakes of previous lives, and ultimately transcend the cycle of birth and death. Karma also brings with it the notion of personal responsibility, as it places the power of transformation in the hands of the individual. In the context of reincarnation, it is not the external world or the will of the divine that dictates our fate, but the choices we make in alignment with our true nature. In this way, karma is intimately tied to the concept of free will—the ability of the soul to choose its path, learn, evolve, and ultimately realize its oneness with the divine. The soul's journey through reincarnation is, therefore, not random or arbitrary, but a conscious unfolding of divine wisdom. Each life is seen as a stepping stone toward ultimate realization and freedom. The process of reincarnation is not solely defined by the external circumstances of life—whether we are born rich or poor, healthy or ill, in a time of peace or war—but by the deeper lessons embedded in the experience. The true essence of reincarnation is spiritual evolution, where the soul gradually transcends the limitations of the material world and realizes its eternal, divine nature. The eternal self, which underlies all of these cycles of reincarnation, is not the ego or the personality that changes from lifetime to lifetime. Rather, the eternal self is the unchanging essence of consciousness that exists beyond time and space. It is often referred to as the Atman in Hindu philosophy, the True Self in Buddhism, or the Higher Self in Western spiritual traditions.

The eternal self is not bound by the fluctuations of the mind, emotions, or body, but remains constant, unperturbed by the drama of human life. It is the source of all awareness, and it is through this eternal self that the soul experiences all of existence. In this context, reincarnation is seen as the process through which the eternal self gradually comes to recognize its true nature, as it moves through the cycles of life and death. Reincarnation and karma, then, are not separate from the divine, but are part of the soul's process of self-discovery and realization. While the soul may be bound by the illusions of individuality and separation in each lifetime, its ultimate goal is to awaken to its oneness with the source of all life, transcending the karmic wheel of reincarnation and returning to the state of pure, undifferentiated consciousness. Many spiritual traditions speak of the liberation or enlightenment that occurs when the soul breaks free from the cycle of reincarnation. In Buddhism, this state is known as nirvana—the extinguishing of desire, ignorance, and suffering, where the individual self dissolves into the universal consciousness. In Hinduism, it is called moksha, the realization of the self's true nature as part of the infinite, eternal Brahman. In Christian mysticism, a similar idea of divine union is expressed through the concept of salvation, where the soul reunites with God after transcending the cycles of earthly life. Although the paths to liberation vary across traditions, the common thread remains: the soul's journey is one of self-realization, healing, and awakening to its ultimate nature, which is boundless and eternal. The notion of life after life—through reincarnation, karma, and the eternal self—offers a profound way of understanding the purpose of existence and the nature of the soul's evolution. Far from being a simple cycle of rebirths, reincarnation is the process by which the soul learns to navigate the challenges of life, heal past wounds, and align itself with the higher truths of existence. The law of karma ensures that every action has consequences, but it also holds the promise of redemption and transformation. No soul is ever truly lost or abandoned in its journey, as every lifetime is an opportunity for growth and healing.

Ultimately, the journey of reincarnation is not a burden, but a divine opportunity for the soul to shed its illusions, transcend its attachments, and realize the eternal, unchanging truth of its own divine essence. This truth is the core of the spiritual quest: the realization that we are not the body, the mind, or the personality, but the eternal self that exists beyond birth and death, beyond time and space. Life after life is not merely a repetition of suffering or struggle but a journey toward liberation, where the soul awakens to its highest potential and reunites with the infinite source of all existence. It is through understanding the laws of reincarnation and karma that we begin to see the true nature of our existence—not as separate individuals lost in a world of illusion, but as eternal souls on a divine journey back to the source of all creation.

ᐒᐒᐒ

Let us see a short story related to this.

In a distant land, where the mountains kissed the skies and the rivers sang of ancient wisdom, there lived a wise sage named Sahasra. Sahasra was known far and wide for her deep understanding of the mysteries of life and death. People came from all corners of the world to seek her guidance, hoping to find answers to the eternal questions that had plagued humanity for millennia: What happens after we die? Is there an end to suffering? What is the purpose of life?

Sahasra lived in a small village, nestled at the foot of a great mountain known as Vishwastara—the Mountain of the Eternal Soul. The villagers believed that Vishwastara was a sacred place, where the souls of the departed would ascend and merge with the divine light. Many spoke of a hidden temple on the mountain's summit, a place said to hold the secret to life's greatest mystery—the truth of reincarnation and karma.

One day, a young man named Aran, filled with grief and confusion, arrived at Sahasra's hut. His face was lined with sorrow, his heart weighed down by the sudden death of his beloved sister, Mira. Desperate for answers, he fell to his knees before the sage.

"O wise Sahasra," he cried, "I do not understand. Mira was young, full of life. Why was her life taken so soon? What happens to her now? Does she simply cease to exist?"

Sahasra smiled gently and beckoned Aran to sit beside her. The air around them hummed with an ancient, silent wisdom, and the sage's eyes seemed to peer beyond time itself.

"Aran," she said softly, "your sorrow is a reflection of the veil that shrouds the truth. Death is not an end, but a transition—a return to the source from which we all come. We are but travelers on a long journey, bound to the wheel of life, death, and rebirth. The soul is eternal, and it continues its journey, lifetime after lifetime, seeking wisdom and understanding."

Aran looked at her with confusion in his eyes. "But if the soul is eternal, why must it endure such suffering? Why is there pain and loss in this world?"

Sahasra nodded knowingly, her voice calm yet profound. "The pain you feel is part of the journey of the soul, Aran. Every soul comes into this world with a purpose—a lesson to learn, a karmic debt to clear, or a desire to transcend. The law of karma governs this process. Every action, every thought, every word creates an imprint on the soul. The choices we make shape the course of our lives, and the consequences of those choices ripple through time, affecting not just us, but all beings we encounter."

"But my sister was kind," Aran protested. "She did no harm to anyone."

"True," Sahasra agreed, "but karma is not always about the immediate actions of a single life. It stretches across lifetimes. Sometimes, what we experience in this life is a result of choices made long ago—choices made by the soul in previous incarnations. The soul's journey is not linear; it is cyclical. Each life is an opportunity for growth, healing, and spiritual evolution. The lessons of this life may not be understood fully in the moment, but they are part of a greater cosmic tapestry, woven across time."

Aran sat in silence, his mind racing with thoughts of his sister. "So you are saying that her death was not a punishment, but part of her soul's journey?"

"Yes," Sahasra replied gently. "And it is part of yours as well. We are all interconnected. What happens to one affects the many, and through our actions, thoughts, and intentions, we create ripples that extend far beyond this lifetime. The pain you feel is a reflection of your own attachments, but in time, you will come to understand that this loss is not the end. It is simply a turning of the page in the story of your soul's journey."

Aran's heart grew heavy with the weight of Sahasra's words, but as he sat in stillness beside her, something shifted within him. A deep sense of peace began to settle over him, and a flicker of understanding began to take root.

Sahasra continued, "Reincarnation is not a random process, Aran. It is a sacred cycle, a path of spiritual evolution. With *each lifetime, the soul is presented with opportunities to learn, to resolve past karmic debts, to release attachments, and to grow in wisdom. And once the soul has transcended the cycle of birth and death, it returns to its true, unchanging nature—a nature of pure consciousness, eternal and boundless."*

Aran's mind wandered back to his sister. "Will Mira be reborn?" he asked quietly.

"She may be," Sahasra answered, "but it will not be the same Mira you knew. The soul sheds its form, just as a snake sheds its skin. Each incarnation is an opportunity for the soul to evolve, to experience new aspects of life and existence. In one life, a soul may be a scholar, in another, a farmer, in another, a king or a beggar. But the soul remains the same—the eternal essence that experiences it all."

Aran sat for a long time, lost in thought. The pain of his sister's death still lingered in his heart, but Sahasra's words gave him a new perspective. Slowly, he began to understand that his grief was not a sign of separation, but a reflection of his deep connection to Mira's soul—a connection that transcended time and space.

As the days passed, Sahasra guided Aran deeper into the teachings of reincarnation and karma, helping him understand that the soul's journey was one of constant learning and evolution. She taught him that the suffering of this life, while painful, was not meaningless. It was part of a larger plan, a *process of spiritual growth that would ultimately lead to liberation from the cycle of birth and death.*

But Sahasra also imparted a key lesson to Aran, one that would forever change the way he viewed the world: the true nature of the soul is love. When one aligns their actions with love, when they act with compassion, kindness, and understanding, they create positive karma, which brings them closer to liberation. It was through the cultivation of love in every moment that the soul could transcend its attachments and realize its oneness with the divine.

Years passed, and Aran became a wise teacher in his own right. He shared the teachings of Sahasra with others, guiding them on their own journeys of self-discovery and spiritual growth. And though the pain of his sister's passing never fully left him, he understood now that her soul was not gone. It had merely moved on to a new chapter in its eternal journey. The love they had shared transcended death, and in every act of kindness, in every moment of compassion, he felt her presence with him, guiding him, always.

*And so, the wheel of life turned. Reincarnation continued its dance of birth, death, and rebirth, as the souls of the departed returned, each carrying the lessons of their past lives into their new ones. **The eternal cycle of karma continued, weaving the tapestry of existence, as souls, like rivers, flowed toward the ocean of divine consciousness, forever evolving, forever seeking.***

NINE

The Power of Presence: Living in the Moment

In a world that is perpetually busy and distracted, the concept of presence—the ability to fully inhabit the moment—is both revolutionary and profoundly simple. The power of presence is the ability to engage with the current moment without the interference of past memories or future anxieties, and it forms the foundation of practices like mindfulness, meditation, and conscious living. This state of presence is not just about being physically in a place, but about being fully aware, connected, and alive in that experience, with a deep sense of awareness of one's thoughts, emotions, and surroundings. At the psychological level, being present can be transformative because it interrupts the habitual patterns of the mind, which are often consumed with regrets about the past or worries about the future. Psychologists and neuroscientists alike have demonstrated that the mind has a tendency to gravitate toward these states of rumination or anticipation, which leads to increased levels of stress, anxiety, and dissatisfaction.

Living in the moment, on the other hand, involves cultivating the ability to quiet the mind, focus on the now, and tap into a deeper sense of stillness and peace. When we live fully in the present, we step out of the cycle of reactivity and start to observe our thoughts and emotions with detachment and compassion. This presence allows us to break free from the narratives we have created about who we are, or who we think we should be, and instead experience life in its raw, unfiltered state. Beyond the psychological benefits, the power of presence also has profound spiritual implications. In many spiritual traditions, being present is considered a path to self-realization and enlightenment. In Buddhism, the practice of mindfulness is central to the path of awakening, as it allows the practitioner to become deeply aware of their thoughts, feelings, and actions in each moment. Through this awareness, they are able to transcend the egoic mind and experience a direct connection with the present moment, which is seen as the doorway to enlightenment. Similarly, in Christianity, the idea of "being present" is embodied in the practice of contemplative prayer, which calls on practitioners to be fully open to the divine in the here and now. The moment, in spiritual terms, is where the eternal dwells—it is not separate from the divine but is itself an expression of spiritual truth. To be present is, therefore, to commune with the divine in every moment, recognizing that time is not linear or fragmented but interconnected and sacred. The power of presence allows us to transcend the limitations of the mind, the body, and time itself. The act of living in the moment is, in many ways, a return to the essence of who we are—the timeless self that exists beyond the fluctuations of thought and emotion. When we are truly present, we align ourselves with a deeper, more expansive reality. We experience a sense of interconnectedness with all things, as our attention is freed from the distractions of the past and future, and we are able to witness the unfolding of life as it is, without judgment or expectation. This practice, however, is not always easy. The mind is constantly moving between thoughts, projections, and evaluations. It takes intentional practice to slow down, quiet the mind, and bring ourselves into the here and now.

Yet, as we do so, we begin to notice profound shifts in our perception. The act of simply being present can lead to greater peace, joy, and clarity, as we stop fighting against the current moment and allow life to unfold naturally. Furthermore, living in the moment transforms how we experience relationships, work, and our daily tasks. When we are fully present, we bring our full attention to others, which fosters deeper connections and understanding. In contrast, when our attention is divided or consumed by distractions, relationships can feel fragmented or superficial.

Presence allows us to show up fully for those we care about, to listen deeply, and to respond with genuine empathy. In the workplace, presence leads to greater productivity, creativity, and satisfaction because we are able to give our best in every task, without the interference of distractions or self-doubt. Rather than rushing through life, the practice of living in the moment encourages us to savor each experience, to find richness in the ordinary, and to acknowledge the inherent value of the present. On a larger scale, the power of presence can transform the way we view time itself. Most of us are conditioned to see time as something finite and precious, always slipping away from us, which leads to a sense of urgency and pressure. The truth, however, is that the present moment is all we truly have. It is in the present that we experience the fullness of life; the past is merely a collection of memories, and the future is unknown and uncertain. When we allow ourselves to be fully present, we let go of the constant pressure to "do" and instead embrace the inherent value of "being." This shift from striving to simply being allows us to cultivate deeper levels of inner peace and acceptance. Through the power of presence, we begin to realize that the only true moment is the one we are currently experiencing. In this way, presence becomes an antidote to the stress and anxiety of modern life. It helps us break free from the mental traps of worrying about the future or regretting the past, and instead ground ourselves in the timeless flow of the present. At its core, living in the moment is an act of liberation. It is liberation from the tyranny of the mind, the endless cycle of craving and aversion, and the illusion of separation. It is a return to a more authentic way of being—one that is fully engaged with life as it unfolds, one that is deeply aware of the sacredness of each moment.

To live in the moment is to accept life as it is, with all its beauty and imperfection, without trying to manipulate or control it. This practice is transformative not just on an individual level, but on a collective one. When more people live in the present, free from the burdens of time and the endless distractions of modern life, the world itself becomes more peaceful, compassionate, and harmonious. The power of presence, then, is not simply a personal practice; it is a spiritual and societal shift that has the potential to radically change the way we experience life. It allows us to see the world with fresh eyes, to connect with others on a deeper level, and to engage with our true selves. In this way, the present moment becomes a portal to transformation—a gateway to experiencing life more fully, more richly, and more authentically.

ᐩᐩᐩ

Let us see a short story related to this.

In a faraway kingdom, nestled between the peaks of towering mountains, there was a mystical garden known as the Garden of the Eternal Moment. It was said that the garden held the key to the greatest treasure of all: the power of presence. Anyone who could walk through its gates and stay fully present in the moment would be granted the wisdom to live without the chains of time—free from the distractions of past regrets and future worries.

The garden was not open to just anyone. It was guarded by an ancient gatekeeper, a wise old man named Zhen, who had lived for countless years. His beard was long and silver, and his eyes sparkled with a quiet knowing, as if he understood the rhythm of the universe itself. Many travellers had come to seek the garden's secret, but few had ever made it through the gate.

One day, three weary wanderers arrived at the garden's entrance: a young warrior named Arjuna, a wandering monk named Bodhi, and a sorrowful queen named Leila. Each of them had heard whispers of the garden's magic and sought its wisdom for different reasons.

Arjuna, the warrior, had spent his life battling enemies on the battlefield. His heart was heavy with the weight of countless wars and victories. He carried the scars of both physical and emotional wounds. Though he had achieved great renown, he felt an emptiness within him—a longing for peace that no victory could bring. His mind was always racing, caught between the ghosts of past battles and the fears of future wars.

Bodhi, the monk, had spent years meditating in the mountains, seeking enlightenment. His heart was pure, and his practice was disciplined, yet there was something elusive about his peace. He could quiet his mind in moments of deep meditation, but when he stepped into the world, he found himself caught in the distractions of everyday life. Despite his deep desire for presence, his mind often wandered, carried away by fleeting thoughts and worries.

Leila, the queen, was burdened by a crown that weighed heavily on her soul. She ruled a vast kingdom, but her heart was torn by the choices she had to make every day. Her life was full of duties, obligations, and expectations. She longed for a moment of true clarity, a moment where she could feel connected to the world without the constant pressures of leadership, the constant worry about the future of her people, and the unspoken grief of lost loved ones.

The three travellers stood before Zhen, each silently hoping that the garden would provide the answers they sought. Zhen greeted them with a warm smile and gestured to the gate behind him.

"Welcome," he said. "The garden is open to all who seek the truth, but remember, the truth cannot be grasped by the mind alone. You must enter with an open heart and a willingness to be present to each moment as it comes."

Arjuna, eager to find peace, stepped forward first. He believed that the answers lay in conquering his fears, but he soon found that each step in the garden seemed to lead him further into the maze of his own mind. He was haunted by memories of the battlefield—faces of the fallen, the cries of the wounded. His thoughts raced ahead to future wars, imagining enemies who might rise to challenge him. With each passing moment, he found it harder to stay in the present. Zhen observed Arjuna's struggles with compassion. "Warrior," he said, "you are a master of many battles, but the greatest battle is within. The past has already passed, and the future has not yet arrived. If you wish to find peace, you must let go of your fear and your desire for control. The present is all you truly have."

Arjuna bowed his head, realizing that his mind had been a battlefield of its own. He began to let go, taking slow breaths and bringing his awareness back to the present moment. Slowly, his thoughts quieted, and he began to feel a peace that had eluded him for so long.

Next, Bodhi, the monk, stepped forward. He had trained his mind to be still, but he was still caught in the patterns of his *thoughts. As he walked deeper into the garden, he found himself reflecting on the teachings of the Buddha, the nature of suffering, and the path to enlightenment. Yet, even in the most serene part of the garden, his mind remained restless, like a butterfly fluttering from one flower to the next.*

Zhen approached Bodhi with a knowing look. "Monk, you have travelled far too quiet your mind, but even in stillness, your mind remains caught in the web of thoughts. True presence is not about escaping the mind but being aware of it as it is. Do not seek to control or silence the thoughts—simply observe them and let them pass. Each thought, each feeling, is like a cloud in the sky. Let them float by without attachment."

Bodhi closed his eyes and began to breathe deeply, observing his thoughts without judgment. As he did, he felt a profound shift. The thoughts came, but they no longer controlled him. He was simply the observer. Slowly, the tension in his mind eased, and a deep sense of presence filled his being.

Finally, Queen Leila, weary from her burdens, entered the garden. She had carried the weight of the kingdom for so long that it had become a part of her. Her heart was heavy with grief for those she had lost and with worry for those she still governed. She walked through the garden's pathways, thinking of her people, of her duties, and of the endless demands on her time.

Zhen spoke gently, "Queen, you carry the weight of the world, but in your heart, there is a deeper truth. The world is always changing, and the crown you wear will one day be passed to another. But the present moment is eternal. It is in this moment that you will find your true sovereignty—not in the future, not in the past, but right here, right now."

Leila paused, letting the words settle into her heart. She began to breathe deeply, letting go of the future that worried her and the past that haunted her. Slowly, the tension in her shoulders eased, and she felt a profound stillness. She understood that her true power came not from her crown, but from her ability to be fully present in the moment, to lead with clarity and compassion, free from the burdens of time.

And so, the three travellers—Arjuna, Bodhi, and Leila—each experienced the transformative power of presence. They realized that the present moment was not just a fleeting point in time, but a portal to the eternal. The wisdom of the garden was simple yet profound: to be fully present was to live in harmony with the universe, to let go of the past and future, and to embrace life in all its raw beauty.

Zhen smiled as he watched them. "Now you understand," he said. "The garden does not offer the wisdom of the ages, for it is the wisdom of the moment. Each moment is the gateway to the divine, and when you are truly present, you are one with all that is."

The three travellers left the garden, forever changed. They returned to their lives, but with a new understanding: they no longer sought the future or regretted the past. They had found the peace and clarity they had longed for, and it resided in the **simple act of being present** in each moment.

TEN

SPIRITUAL PRACTICES ACROSS CULTURES: A UNIVERSAL TRUTH

Across time and geography, spiritual practices have emerged in diverse cultures and civilizations, each reflecting a unique expression of humanity's search for meaning, connection, and transcendence. Despite the apparent differences in rituals, symbols, and deities, there is a deep underlying unity in the spiritual traditions of the world. From the mystical devotion of Sufism in the Middle East to the meditation practices of Buddhism in the East, from the contemplative silence of Christian monasticism to the ecstatic dance of indigenous ceremonies, each tradition points to a common truth: the human spirit is intrinsically connected to a larger, universal consciousness or divine source. This shared aim—union with the divine, self-realization, or enlightenment—forms the backbone of spiritual practice, regardless of cultural context. While the methods may vary, the end goal remains remarkably similar: to awaken the individual to a deeper understanding of their purpose, to experience a direct connection with the sacred, and to transcend the limitations of the ego in order to embody a state of pure awareness, love, and compassion. For instance, in Hinduism, the practice of *yoga* is a holistic system designed to unite the mind, body, and spirit with the Divine, through disciplines such as meditation (*dhyana*), devotion (*bhakti*), and selfless action (*karma yoga*).

In Buddhism, the path to enlightenment is deeply intertwined with practices such as mindfulness (sati) and meditation (zazen), which are designed to cultivate awareness, promote inner peace, and overcome attachment to the material world. Through mindfulness, practitioners learn to observe their thoughts, emotions, and sensations without judgment, allowing them to detach from the ego and the illusions that cause suffering. Meditation further aids in deepening this awareness, helping to quiet the mind and achieve the state of Nirvana—a liberation from the cycle of suffering, craving, and illusion. Similarly, in indigenous cultures across Africa, the Americas, and Oceania, spiritual practices are centred on rituals, songs, drumming, and dances that establish a profound connection with the Earth, ancestors, and the forces of nature. These practices reflect an understanding of the sacredness of life and the belief that humans are intricately woven into the fabric of the natural world. In many of these traditions, spirituality is not an abstract pursuit, but a grounded, embodied practice that seeks to align individuals with the rhythms of the Earth, the seasons, and the cycles of life and death. Native American ceremonies, such as the sweat lodge and the Sun Dance, exemplify this connection, offering rituals of purification and renewal that serve to restore balance and promote personal transformation. These sacred ceremonies are seen as opportunities for deep introspection, healing, and spiritual renewal, emphasizing the importance of living in harmony with nature and acknowledging the sacredness of the world around us. Whether through meditation and mindfulness or through ritualistic practices that engage the body and spirit, these diverse spiritual paths highlight a common theme: a return to a deeper awareness of our connection to the Earth and to the unseen forces that govern the universe, providing powerful pathways to healing, enlightenment, and spiritual awakening.

In the Western spiritual tradition, mystics and philosophers have long pointed to universal truths through deep practices of introspection, prayer, and contemplation, using these tools as pathways to understanding the divine and the soul's ultimate purpose. Christian mystics like John of the Cross and Teresa of Ávila offer profound insights into the transformative journey of the soul, emphasizing the power of silence and prayer in attaining union with God. For John of the Cross, the soul's journey is a process of purification, one that often involves intense trials like the Dark Night of the Soul, in which the individual feels abandoned by God. However, this spiritual dryness is not a punishment but a crucial phase in which the soul is stripped of worldly attachments and ego, allowing it to reach a state of true humility and receptivity to God's love. John teaches that divine love is transformative, not only in its capacity to heal and purify but also in its ability to unite the soul with God, transcending the limitations of the individual self. Similarly, Teresa of Ávila, in her mystical work The Interior Castle, illustrates the soul's journey toward God through a series of concentric rooms, each representing deeper stages of spiritual growth. The innermost room symbolizes the direct experience of God, which can only be accessed through prayer, silence, and an open, humble heart. For Teresa, prayer is not merely a recitation of words but a transformative practice that opens the soul to divine presence, enabling a profound union with God. In both mystics' writings, there is an emphasis on inner silence and detachment from the material world as essential elements for spiritual awakening. This detachment, however, is not an escape from the world but an immersion into a deeper, more sacred reality, where the soul can experience the fullness of divine love. Both mystics highlight that the ultimate goal of spiritual practice is not intellectual knowledge or external achievement, but a radical transformation of the self, achieved through love and surrender to God. They teach that through the practices of prayer, contemplation, and silence, the soul undergoes a process of refinement, where ego and self-centeredness are replaced with divine love and grace. In this process, the individual not only draws closer to God but also contributes to the collective spiritual awakening of humanity, embodying the transformative power of divine presence in the world. Through the writings and teachings of John of the Cross and Teresa of Ávila, the mystical tradition reveals that true spiritual fulfilment is found in surrendering to love—both divine and human—and that through love, the soul can experience its deepest union with God, transcending the boundaries of the self and entering into the infinite, ever-present reality of divine communion.

In Judaism, the mystical tradition of Kabbalah explores the esoteric and hidden dimensions of the sacred texts, particularly the Torah, aiming to uncover the deeper truths of creation and the nature of God. Kabbalists believe that by studying the divine mysteries encoded in the texts and through esoteric practices like meditation, prayer, and sacred rituals, one can come closer to an experiential understanding of God's presence and the workings of the universe. Central to Kabbalah is the idea of the Tree of Life, a diagram representing the structure of creation and the divine emanations through which God interacts with the world. By contemplating these teachings, practitioners seek to ascend spiritually, gaining access to hidden knowledge and realizing the interconnectedness of all things. For Kabbalists, spiritual practice is not merely about intellectual understanding but involves a transformation of the heart and soul, where meditation and reflection bring the individual into a deeper alignment with divine wisdom and a clearer awareness of their own place in the cosmic order.

The common thread in all these spiritual traditions is the understanding that spiritual practice is a means of transformation. Across religions and cultures, spiritual practices serve to transform the individual from a state of ignorance, ego-driven desires, and suffering, into one of enlightenment, selflessness, and divine connection. In Buddhism, for example, the Four Noble Truths outline the nature of suffering and the path to its cessation through mindfulness, meditation, and ethical living, while the Eightfold Path offers practical guidelines for living in harmony with the dharma, or universal truth. The goal is to strip away the illusions that bind the mind, purify the heart, and attain the ultimate freedom of Nirvana—a state of liberation from the cycle of suffering and ignorance. Similarly, in Christian mysticism, the transformative practices of prayer and contemplation seek to bring the soul into union with God, experiencing divine love and the presence of the Holy Spirit. Practices such as fasting, pilgrimage, and sacred rites in Islam, Christianity, and Judaism also aim to purify the body and spirit, leading the individual toward a deeper communion with the Divine. In indigenous cultures, more spontaneous expressions like ecstatic dance or rituals of drumming and chanting serve as a means of entering altered states of consciousness, where the practitioner can experience the divine presence in nature and reconnect with ancestral wisdom. These rituals, whether structured or spontaneous, share a common purpose: to strip away the layers of illusion that obscure the true nature of the self, helping individuals realize their inherent oneness with the Divine and the universe. Whether through disciplined meditation, prayer, fasting, or ecstatic rituals, the aim is to move beyond the ego, transcend worldly attachments, and awaken to the unity of all life—leading the practitioner toward spiritual enlightenment and a deeper sense of interconnectedness with all beings.

Across cultures, these spiritual practices emphasize the cultivation of virtues like compassion, love, humility, and forgiveness—qualities that are universally recognized as essential for spiritual growth. They also underscore the importance of discipline and devotion, whether through the daily observance of rituals, the commitment to a particular spiritual path, or the dedication to the welfare of others. While these practices differ in their outward forms, they all point to an inner transformation that transcends the individual self. In this way, spirituality, in all its forms, offers a map for navigating the complexities of life, a way of making sense of human suffering, and a pathway toward ultimate freedom and enlightenment. The universal truth of spirituality, as expressed through the vast array of spiritual practices across cultures, is that the divine is not something external to us, but rather something that resides within us. It is in the cultivation of inner awareness and the surrender of the ego that we come to know our true nature—our connection to the divine sparks that is the source of all life. As the Buddha famously said, "You are the light of the world," and through the practice of awakening to this inner light, we can begin to see the divine presence in all things, in all people, and in all of existence. Whether through the path of devotion in Hinduism, the practice of mindfulness in Buddhism, the ecstatic union in Sufism, or the contemplative prayer of Christianity, the aim remains the same: to recognize the sacredness of life, the interconnectedness of all beings, and our place in the grand, cosmic design. The practices, no matter how diverse, serve as tools to strip away the illusions that prevent us from experiencing our true nature and to reveal the universal truth that resides within us all: we are not separate from the divine; we are the divine in expression.

ϸϸϸ

Let us see a short story related to this.

Once, in a land where mountains touched the sky and rivers wove through forests like veins of the earth, there lived four travelers. They were bound by a single purpose: to seek the source of all wisdom and to discover the true nature of their own being. Though they came from distant corners of the world, each carrying the wisdom of their respective traditions, their hearts shared a common longing: the desire for spiritual awakening.

The first was Seema, a yogi from the East, whose practice of yoga and meditation had led him to understand that the true self, or Atman, was beyond the body, mind, and ego. Through deep concentration and the discipline of the breath, he had come to experience moments of profound stillness, where he felt at one with the vast universe. Yet, he knew that his journey was far from over. There was a deeper truth he had yet to grasp.

The second was Miriam, a mystic from the West, whose life was devoted to contemplative prayer and silence. She had spent years in the solitude of a Christian monastery, seeking union with the Divine through the path of humility, surrender, and love. She believed that the soul's journey was one of purification, where the ego must be surrendered so that the soul could be bathed in the infinite love of God. But despite her deep faith, a question lingered in her heart: Could she ever truly experience the Divine presence without losing herself in the process?

The third was Jamil, a Sufi poet and dancer, whose ecstatic dances and songs had brought him closer to the Divine. He knew the path of love and longing, where every step and every breath were offerings to the Beloved. Through the whirling dance of the Dervish, he sought to transcend the limitations of his earthly body and to unite with the infinite spirit of God. But even in his ecstasy, he wondered: What is the source of the love that moves him, and where does it lead?

The fourth was Nahua, an elder from a Native American tribe, who had lived most of his life in close communion with the earth. His people revered the land, the animals, and the forces of nature as sacred. Through the rituals of drumming, chanting, and dancing, they sought to connect with the spirits of their ancestors and the natural world, believing that everything in existence was a manifestation of the Creator's divine will. Nahua had seen visions during his sacred sweat lodge ceremonies, and in his dreams, the spirits spoke to him. Yet he too felt the pull of a deeper mystery, one that bound him to the stars and to the unseen world.

One fateful day, their paths converged in a remote valley, where a vast tree stood at the center of a sacred grove. It was said that the tree was the Tree of Life, the origin of all wisdom, and the portal to the divine. Each of them had heard the call to come here, though none of them knew how or why. All that was known was that the answers they sought lay beneath the tree's ancient roots. As they stood together beneath the mighty tree, each felt the weight of their individual quests. Seema, with his disciplined meditation, Miriam, with her prayerful silence,

Jamil, with his ecstatic dance, and Nahua, with his connection to the earth—all stood facing the same question: What is the source of all wisdom, the ultimate truth of existence?

The tree whispered in a language none of them could understand, and yet, all felt the meaning of its words deep within their hearts.

Seemay, the yogi, stepped forward first. He closed his eyes and sat in lotus posture, his hands resting gently on his knees. He began to breathe deeply, bringing his awareness inward. In his meditation, he felt the vastness of the universe and the silence that underlies all of existence. He heard the tree's voice as a gentle vibration in the very depths of his being, saying, "The truth you seek is not outside, but within. The divine is in the stillness, in the space between your thoughts, where all distinctions dissolve."

Miriam, the mystic, knelt beside the tree and began to pray. She poured out her heart, asking for the Divine to reveal the truth to her. In the silence that followed her prayer, she felt a warmth envelop her, a love that transcended all words. The tree whispered to her in a voice as soft as the wind, "The soul's journey is one of love and surrender. The ego must dissolve in the presence of love, for only through love can the soul find union with the Divine."

Jamil, the Sufi poet, began to spin in the sacred dance, his arms outstretched, his heart open to the Beloved. As he whirled in ecstatic devotion, he felt a deep connection to the earth beneath him and the sky above. The tree spoke to him as he danced, saying, "In love, you transcend the boundaries of the self. The dance of life is a prayer, a longing for the One. Through love and devotion, you return to the source of all creation."

Finally, Nahua, the elder, took a handful of earth from the ground and held it to his heart. He closed his eyes and listened to the beating of his own heart, feeling the pulse of life all around him. In the stillness of the earth, he heard the tree's voice, deep and ancient, saying, "You are the earth, the sky, the stars, and the wind. All things are interconnected in the sacred web of life.

The Creator dwells in every living being, in every breath, in every heartbeat. To know the Creator is to know yourself." As each of the travelers listened to the tree's wisdom, they began to understand. The truth they sought was not separate, but one.

Whether through the stillness of meditation, the surrender of prayer, the devotion of dance, or the connection to the earth, all paths led to the same destination: union with the Divine, self-realization, and a deep recognition of the interconnectedness of all things.

Seemay, Miriam, Jamil, and Nahua stood together in silence, united in their understanding. They realized that their separate traditions were but different expressions of the same truth, like rivers that all flowed into the same ocean.

The yoga, the prayer, the dance, the rituals—they were all ways to strip away the illusion of separation and to awaken to the divine presence that resided within them and in all things. And so, in the shadow of the Tree of Life, they vowed to continue their journey—not as separate seekers, but as one, **knowing that the divine was not outside them, but within**, and that the path to enlightenment was not a destination, but a continual unfolding of the truth of who they truly were.

ELEVEN

THE QUEST FOR ENLIGHTENMENT: THE PURPOSE OF HUMAN EXISTENCE

The quest for enlightenment—understood as the profound awakening to one's true nature—is the most fundamental pursuit of human existence. Across cultures, philosophies, and spiritual traditions, the idea of enlightenment has held a central role, shaping not only religious thought but also the broader quest for meaning and purpose in life. Whether framed as moksha in Hinduism, nirvana in Buddhism, salvation in Christianity, or the realization of the True Self in various mystical paths, enlightenment represents the ultimate liberation from the limitations of the ego, suffering, and the illusion of separateness. It is the realization that our true nature is not bound by time, space, or material forms, but is an eternal, boundless consciousness that is interconnected with all of existence. In this sense, the purpose of human existence is not to accumulate wealth, power, or personal achievement, but to awaken to this deeper, underlying truth—an awareness of the divine essence within oneself and within all beings. This journey toward enlightenment is inherently spiritual but has profound psychological and existential implications as well. The human mind, conditioned by the stories it tells about itself, the attachments it forms, and the fears it nurtures, becomes trapped in cycles of suffering and illusion. Enlightenment, then, can be understood as the process of transcending the ego—those false identities we construct in order to cope with the challenges and complexities of life. These identities, based on attachment to physical possessions, societal roles, and transient experiences, bind us to a limited and fragmented sense of self. The purpose of human existence, then, becomes a process of remembering who we truly are beyond these ephemeral layers, and uncovering the inherent unity that lies at the heart of all creation. It is a spiritual path that calls for surrender—to let go of the need to control, to resist, or to impose our will on the world. Through surrender, we learn to live with greater acceptance, compassion, and awareness, realizing that the moment we are living in is the only moment that exists, and that our very existence is an expression of the divine. Enlightenment, therefore, is not a distant goal or a final destination but a continuous unfolding of truth, a deepening understanding of our interconnectedness with all beings. The most profound question in human life is not "What do I want to achieve?" but "Who am I, beyond all roles, beyond all labels, beyond all of the transient experiences I identify with?" This question leads us on a journey of self-inquiry and introspection, where we strip away the layers of conditioning, trauma, and ignorance that obscure our true nature.

While many spiritual traditions suggest various practices to attain enlightenment—be it through meditation, prayer, selfless action, or devotion—there is a universal recognition that awakening cannot be forced, nor can it be acquired through external means. It is, ultimately, the realization that the truth we seek is already within us, waiting to be uncovered. In this light, the purpose of human existence shifts from striving for external validation to an inward quest for self-discovery and spiritual growth. However, this journey is not without its challenges. Enlightenment requires not only personal transformation but a profound shift in how we perceive the world. It calls for us to look beyond the surface of things and recognize the deeper, unseen patterns that bind us all together. Enlightenment, therefore, is not just a personal experience, but one that has the potential to transform the world around us. As individuals awaken to their divine nature, the ripple effect of this awareness can lead to greater harmony, peace, and compassion in society. In this sense, the quest for enlightenment also becomes the quest for collective healing and unity. Each step toward awakening is a step toward breaking down the walls of separation that create division and conflict. In this light, the purpose of human existence is not only about individual liberation but also about contributing to the collective awakening of humanity as a whole. This collective shift in consciousness will ultimately lead us to a greater understanding of the unity of all beings, transcending racial, cultural, and ideological divides. To experience enlightenment is to experience the oneness of all life—the recognition that there is no "other," only a shared essence that connects all people, animals, and nature itself. Enlightenment, in this way, becomes a radical act of love, a return to a state of purity, innocence, and joy that has been buried beneath the layers of conditioning and suffering. The journey of enlightenment is the journey back to the Source, the Divine, or whatever name we use to describe the ultimate reality. It is a process of reconnecting with the sacredness of life, recognizing that everything in the universe is an expression of the same divine consciousness. As we awaken to this truth, we no longer view the world through the lens of duality—good versus bad, right versus wrong, self-versus other—but through the lens of unity, where all distinctions dissolve into the realization that we are one with all that is. The ultimate purpose of human existence, then, is to realize this profound truth of oneness, to awaken from the dream of separation, and to live in harmony with the divine order of the universe. This realization is not an intellectual understanding but an experiential shift—a radical reorientation of how we experience and relate to the world. It is a shift from identification with the ego to identification with the soul, from the pursuit of fleeting pleasures and external achievements to the cultivation of inner peace, wisdom, and love. This journey of awakening is the most sacred and transformative journey we can undertake in this life and it is the very reason for our existence: to remember who we are, to realize our true nature, and to experience the oneness of all life in the here and now.

ᐳᐳᐳ

Let us see a short story related to this.

Once, in an ancient kingdom nestled between towering mountains and endless fields of golden grass, there was a humble village at the edge of a great forest. The villagers, though simple in their ways, lived in peace and contentment. But one among them, a young man named Asha, felt a restlessness that could not be quieted by the rhythms of daily life. He had heard stories of a mystical place known as the Lotus of the Endless Sky, a place where the very essence of the universe was said to be revealed to those who sought it with pure hearts.

Asha had spent many years in meditation, in the company of wise elders, and in deep introspection. Yet, despite all his efforts, he felt that he had not yet touched the true nature of his being. The teachings of the elders spoke of enlightenment, but Asha's heart remained unsettled, as if something vital were always just out of reach. He longed for the experience that would awaken him fully to his true self.

One evening, as the sun dipped below the horizon, an old traveler appeared in the village. With his long, white beard and robes that seemed to shimmer like stardust, he caught Asha's attention. The traveler spoke in a voice that echoed the deep, ancient truths of the earth itself.

"Child, you seek the Lotus of the Endless Sky, do you not?" the traveler asked.

"Yes," Asha replied, his heart racing, "I have heard of it in stories and dreams. But no one has ever returned from it. Is it real?"

The traveler smiled. "The Lotus is not a place, but a truth. It is not found in the world outside but in the stillness of the mind and the depth of the heart. But you must be ready. Your quest is not to find something that has been lost; it is to remember what you already know."

Asha, determined to follow the path of awakening, bid the traveler farewell and set off on his journey. He wandered through dense forests and across vast, desolate deserts, his mind filled with doubts and questions. The path was long and arduous, but Asha pressed forward, driven by a deep yearning for the truth.

One day, after crossing a particularly treacherous mountain pass, Asha came upon a great river. The water was swift and turbulent, and the banks were steep and jagged. As he stood there, wondering how to cross, an old woman appeared, holding a simple wooden staff. Her eyes were wise and clear, as though she had seen the beginning and end of time itself.

"*Do you seek the Lotus of the Endless Sky?*" she asked, her voice gentle but firm.

"*Yes,*" Asha answered. "*But I cannot cross this river. How can I continue my journey?*"

The woman looked at him kindly. "*The river is the mind,*" she said. "*The current is your thoughts, rushing in every direction. You cannot cross it while you are caught in its flow. You must learn to still your mind, to surrender to the current, not fight it. Only then will the way become clear.*"

Asha stood in silence for a long time, contemplating her words. Finally, he closed his eyes and took a deep breath. With *each exhale, he let go of his thoughts, his fears, his desires. Gradually, he felt his mind calm, as if the river's tumultuous waves had subsided into stillness. When he opened his eyes again, the river no longer seemed an obstacle; it had transformed into a calm, shimmering reflection of the sky above. He crossed it easily, his steps light, as if the very earth itself was supporting him.*

Further along his journey, Asha met another sage—this one a young monk who lived in a secluded temple atop a mountain. The monk was known for his wisdom and serenity, and Asha sought his guidance.

"I have learned to still the mind," Asha said, "but I still feel as if something is missing. How can I truly know the truth of my being?"

The monk smiled, his eyes gleaming with a quiet knowing. "The truth is not a concept to be understood, nor a goal to be reached. It is the essence of your very existence. You seek it as though it is separate from you, but in reality, you are already one with it."

"But how can that be?" Asha asked, his brow furrowing in confusion. "I feel separate from everything, distant from the universe."

The monk reached into his robes and pulled out a simple lotus flower. He held it out to Asha, who took it in his hands with reverence. "This flower," the monk explained, "grows in the mud, yet its petals remain untouched by it. It is a symbol of enlightenment: the realization that you are not the mud, nor the water, nor the heat of the sun—but the lotus itself. You are the pure consciousness that witnesses all things, unchanging and eternal."

Asha gazed at the flower, and for a moment, something within him shifted. He saw the petals of the lotus not as separate from him, but as an expression of the same essence that flowed through his own being. The realization came gently, like the unfolding of a bloom in the quiet of the dawn.

In that moment, Asha understood. He was not separate from the world around him, nor was he defined by his thoughts, his desires, or his fears. His true nature was boundless, beyond time and form, a timeless consciousness that flowed through all things. The illusion of separation had dissolved, and in its place was the vast, unbroken unity of existence.

Asha continued his journey, now not as a seeker but as one who had found. He returned to his village, where the people saw a profound change in him. No longer did he speak of seeking enlightenment, for he knew it was not something to be attained—it was the very essence of who he was, always present and unchanging beneath the layers of illusion.

*He lived the rest of his days as an embodiment of peace, wisdom, and love, sharing the simple truth of his realization with all who came to him. And when his time came to leave this world, it was not with fear or regret, but with a deep sense of gratitude, for he knew that he was the **Lotus of the Endless Sky—eternal, boundless, and one with all that is.***

TWELVE

LIVING WITH AWARENESS: INTEGRATING SPIRITUALITY INTO DAILY LIFE

Living with awareness, or integrating spirituality into daily life, is the profound practice of aligning every thought, action, and interaction with the deep awareness of our interconnectedness to all things, to the divine, and to the essence of existence itself. This way of living is not confined to formal spiritual practices, such as prayer, meditation, or rituals, but involves infusing every aspect of daily life with mindfulness, presence, and intentionality. Spirituality, in this context, is not something that can be segmented or compartmentalized to specific times of day or specific actions, but rather something that permeates every aspect of our lives—from how we wake up in the morning to how we engage with others and even how we process our own thoughts and emotions. The practice of living with awareness begins with the recognition that the present moment is all that exists. Spirituality, at its core, teaches us that everything in life is sacred, that divinity is present in the mundane as much as it is in the extraordinary, and that each moment is an opportunity for awakening. The mind, however, is often caught up in the past or future, distracted by thoughts, judgments, and anticipations. The first step in integrating spirituality into daily life is, therefore, to cultivate mindfulness—the practice of bringing our full attention to the present moment, without attachment or aversion. This means being fully present with whatever we are doing, whether it's washing the dishes, engaging in a conversation, driving, or working on a task. Every action becomes an opportunity to practice awareness, to live consciously, and to transcend the habitual patterns of thought that keep us disconnected from the present. In doing so, we cultivate a deeper connection to ourselves, to others, and to the world around us. Mindful living requires the surrender of the egoic mind—the incessant stream of thoughts, desires, and judgments that often prevent us from fully experiencing life as it is. In the space of awareness, we begin to dissolve the boundaries of self and other, seeing the interconnectedness of all beings.

Our interactions with others, for example, become opportunities for practicing compassion and kindness, as we recognize the divinity in everyone we meet. The act of listening deeply to another person, without judgment or distraction, is a spiritual practice in itself—one that fosters empathy and understanding. In the workplace, integrating spirituality into daily life means approaching tasks with a sense of purpose, clarity, and presence. Rather than rushing through the day in a state of anxiety or preoccupation, we can cultivate a mindset of flow, where we are fully immersed in the task at hand. Whether we are making a decision, solving a problem, or simply performing routine duties, the practice of spiritual awareness allows us to approach each moment with a sense of equanimity and openness. Even in moments of stress or difficulty, living with awareness offers the possibility of finding peace in the midst of challenge. Spirituality in daily life teaches us that nothing is inherently separate from the sacred—whether it's work, relationships, or personal struggles. Every aspect of life is an opportunity to express divinity, to show love and kindness, and to be present to the reality of existence as it unfolds. This shift in consciousness is both liberating and transformative, as it allows us to break free from the automatic, reactive patterns of the ego and to live more intentionally and consciously. Furthermore, integrating spirituality into daily life is not just about the internal state of being, but also about the impact it has on our external world. The way we live our daily lives becomes a reflection of our spiritual practices and beliefs. This integration is not about renouncing the world or retreating from ordinary life, but rather about embracing it fully, with a sense of reverence and gratitude. Each moment becomes an opportunity to live in alignment with higher principles—whether it's compassion, patience, humility, or love. In the spiritual tradition of Taoism, for instance, the idea of *wu wei*—action through non-action—emphasizes the power of living in harmony with the flow of life, rather than struggling against it. By learning to be present and accepting in every moment, we allow life to unfold with greater ease, free from unnecessary resistance or striving. Similarly, in Buddhism, the concept of *sunyata* (emptiness) teaches us that everything is interconnected and impermanent. By living with awareness of this interconnectedness, we let go of the need to cling to our own desires, identities, and expectations, and instead cultivate a deep sense of peace and acceptance. The integration of spirituality into daily life requires cultivating inner awareness and transforming the way we engage with the external world. This process of transformation starts with the recognition that everything is interconnected, that our thoughts, words, and actions have an impact on the world around us, and that living with awareness is a pathway to not only personal awakening but also collective healing. Spirituality is not about escapism or transcending the challenges of life, but about awakening to the sacredness of every moment, of seeing the divine in the ordinary, and of living in a state of continuous mindfulness. As we cultivate this awareness in our daily lives, we create a space for deeper insight, inner peace, and a greater capacity for love, both for ourselves and others. The more we practice living with awareness, the more we begin to realize that spirituality is not an isolated, separate part of life, but the very essence of life itself. Through this lens, every action, every moment, every experience becomes an opportunity for spiritual growth. When we live with awareness, we no longer seek meaning outside of ourselves or in distant, abstract goals, but instead find that meaning arises in the present, in our everyday existence. The purpose of life itself becomes an act of continual awareness—embracing the present moment with full presence, love, and compassion. Ultimately, integrating spirituality into daily life allows us to live more fully, more consciously, and with a deeper sense of connection to both the divine and the world around us. It is a practice of awakening that transforms not only our personal experience but also our interactions with others, our work, and our relationships with the planet itself. In this way, spiritual awareness becomes the foundation for a more harmonious, compassionate, and meaningful existence.

ﭏﭏﭏ

Let us see a short story related to this.

Clara sat in her small apartment, the sunlight filtering softly through the curtains, casting warm, golden hues across the room. She had always been a thinker, caught up in the mental swirl of to-do lists, future plans, and worries about what others thought. But for the past few months, something inside her had begun to shift. It started with a book she picked up at a local bookstore—Living with Awareness: Integrating Spirituality into Daily Life. It wasn't just another self-help book, but a deep call to realign her daily actions with a higher sense of presence.

She began to experiment with what it might mean to live more mindfully, to bring spiritual awareness into every corner of her life, no matter how ordinary it seemed.

It was a Saturday morning, and Clara had just woken up. She had set an intention the night before to be fully present throughout the day—no distractions, no rushing, no multitasking. She stood in front of the bathroom mirror, washing her face, feeling the coolness of the water against her skin. Usually, this was just a routine, a blur of action before moving on to the next task. But today, she decided to be fully with the water, fully aware of the sensation, the sound, and the clarity that came with each splash. She realized that in the simple act of washing her face, she could connect with the present moment. The act became sacred in its own right.

As she moved on to breakfast, Clara continued her practice of mindfulness. She made her coffee slowly, feeling each step—grinding the beans, boiling the water, letting the rich aroma fill the air. In the past, her mornings had been a race.

But now, every task felt infused with meaning. She noticed the stillness of the morning, the quiet of the world outside, and the softness of her own breath as she sat at the table, sipping her coffee. Her thoughts would still try to wander, but each time she caught herself, she gently returned to the present moment.

Her mind often raced ahead to future concerns, anxieties about work, relationships, and the general pace of life. But Clara began to realize, as she practiced this awareness, that the future never truly arrived. It was always now, always the present that mattered. She remembered a quote from the book she had read: "The mind is often caught in the past or future, distracted by *thoughts and judgments, but the present moment is all that exists." It resonated deeply with her. Every moment, no matter how mundane, was an opportunity for spiritual awakening.*

Later, she went for a walk in the park. In the past, walking had been nothing more than a way to get exercise or clear her head. But now, as she strolled through the trees, she felt deeply connected to the world around her. The leaves, rustling in the wind, felt like whispers from the universe. The birds' songs were not just noise, but part of the intricate web of existence. She noticed the children playing, the elderly couples chatting, the joggers moving with rhythmic precision. Everyone was part of this intricate dance, this flow of life, and Clara felt deeply honoured to be part of it.

At work, Clara began to notice the small ways in which she could integrate mindfulness into her daily tasks. Her office was often a place of chaos, filled with emails, meetings, and constant deadlines. She had once found herself overwhelmed by the relentless pace. But now, when she sat at her desk, she made an effort to be fully present with each task. Instead of rushing through emails with half her mind on the next thing, she focused on the words in front of her, on the clarity of her responses. Even when a difficult problem arose, she found a calm center within herself, approaching it with the clarity of mind that came from living in the present.

One afternoon, Clara's colleague, David, stopped by her desk to chat. In the past, Clara might have listened distractedly, her thoughts preoccupied with her own issues, trying to think of a way to hurry the conversation along. But today, she decided to be fully present. She listened to David's words, not just with her ears, but with her heart. She felt his struggles, his hopes, and his frustrations. She didn't try to fix him or offer solutions. Instead, she simply offered him compassion—her full presence, undistracted. David seemed to soften, to open up in a way that he hadn't before. It was a moment of connection, and Clara realized that these moments of presence with others were just as sacred as meditation or prayer.

At the end of the day, Clara felt a deep sense of gratitude. As she washed the dishes, a task she had always found tedious, she was once again fully aware. The warm water, the soap, the dishes themselves—they were all part of the sacred flow of life. It was no longer a chore but a moment of quiet reflection. She felt deeply connected to herself and the world around her.

Over time, Clara found that the more she lived with awareness, the more her world opened up. She was no longer a passive participant, caught in the ebb and flow of life's demands. She had become an active, conscious participant in every moment. Whether it was the simple act of cooking dinner, listening to a friend, or responding to an email, each moment became an opportunity for spiritual growth and connection. She had come to understand that spirituality was not about escaping the world or finding peace in some distant future—it was about being fully present with what was before her, seeing the divine in every moment.

One evening, as Clara sat on her balcony, looking out at the sunset, she felt a deep sense of peace. The world was beautiful, and she was part of it. She realized that spirituality had become woven into the fabric of her daily life—not as a set of practices, but as a way of being. Her thoughts, her actions, her words—all were now aligned with a deeper awareness of the interconnectedness of everything.

She closed her eyes, taking a deep breath. In that moment, Clara understood what it meant to live with awareness. It was to live fully, to embrace each moment as sacred, to see the divine in the ordinary, and to be present with everything around her. She had found that the purpose of life was not in some distant goal, but in every breath, every step, and every action.

And as Clara sat there, in the quiet of the evening, she felt a sense of deep gratitude and peace. She had learned to live with awareness, and in doing so, she had unlocked a new way of being—one that was **connected, mindful, and deeply attuned to the sacredness of life** itself.

THIRTEEN

BEYOND THE SELF: THE HIGHER DIMENSIONS OF EXISTENCE

The concept of *self*—the "I" that we so firmly identify with—has been the cornerstone of human experience and understanding for millennia, yet it is often, in essence, a limited and illusory construct. In the everyday experience, the self is shaped by our thoughts, emotions, memories, and the identity we build through culture, family, and personal history. Yet this self is not the true, unchanging essence of who we are. The higher dimensions of existence, accessible through deep spiritual awakening, meditation, and self-inquiry, point toward an existence beyond the ego, beyond the small, finite self that is defined by separateness, time, and circumstance. At the core of many of the world's mystical and philosophical traditions, from Eastern spirituality to Western mysticism, lies the assertion that true enlightenment or awakening occurs when the individual realizes that the egoic self is an illusion, a transient story we tell ourselves. In this awakening, the individual transcends the boundaries of the self and begins to experience a reality that is unified, boundless, and beyond the limited sense of separation. The higher dimensions of existence—whether perceived as higher planes of consciousness, a state of divine unity, or the realization of the interconnectedness of all things—are not abstract philosophical concepts but lived experiences of expanded awareness, where the distinction between self and other, subject and object, disappears.

In these moments of profound clarity, individuals experience what many traditions call *oneness*, a state where they are no longer separate from the universe but realize that their essence is the same as the divine essence that permeates all things. This is what mystics refer to as *self-realization*—the deep understanding that the individual self is not separate but an expression of a larger, cosmic consciousness. Such experiences are described in the mystical traditions of the East, such as in Buddhism's concept of *Nirvana* or Hinduism's *Moksha*, where liberation is not merely freedom from suffering but a return to a state of pure awareness, untainted by the limitations of individual identity. In Christianity, this unity with God is echoed in the concept of the *Kingdom of Heaven* within, where the soul, through grace, reunites with the divine presence. The idea that the self is an illusion is not easily accepted by the ordinary mind, conditioned as it is by the day-to-day realities of survival, desire, and attachment. Yet, it is precisely the limitations of the ego—the attachment to transient forms, to the body, to societal roles, to material gain—that bind us to the cycle of suffering and keep us disconnected from the higher dimensions of existence. In transcending the self, we enter into a state of consciousness where time, space, and even individuality dissolve, and we recognize that all beings and all experiences are interconnected expressions of the same underlying reality. The higher dimensions of existence, then, are not places we go after death, but states of being we can access while still in the body. These states, sometimes referred to as *higher planes of consciousness*, are often described as states of infinite peace, joy, and love, where the individual no longer identifies with the body or the mind but with the essence of pure consciousness itself. These dimensions are not reserved for the saints, sages, or enlightened beings; they are available to all who are willing to look beyond the veil of illusion and let go of the limitations imposed by the ego. Modern science has begun to point in the direction of these higher dimensions as well, through the fields of quantum physics and consciousness studies, which suggest that reality is far more interconnected and multidimensional than the linear, materialistic worldview would have us believe. The higher dimensions of existence, according to quantum theory, may not be separate realms at all, but rather different vibrational frequencies or states of consciousness that coexist in the same space and time. These dimensions can be accessed through deep states of meditation, altered states of awareness, or through intense moments of mystical experience. Beyond the physical world, there is an infinite expanse of non-material reality that cannot be perceived through the five senses, but that is no less real. This understanding aligns with ancient teachings that assert the material world is only one aspect of reality, with many layers or planes of existence beyond it.

To move beyond the self and enter the higher dimensions of existence is not simply an intellectual understanding, but a direct experiential realization. When one transcends the personal self, one begins to experience the world not as an isolated individual, but as part of a greater whole. The world becomes no longer "mine" or "yours," but *ours*—a shared, interconnected, and indivisible reality. The higher dimensions, then, are not separate from the world we live in, but represent the depth and infinite nature of existence that is always present beneath the surface. To access them requires a radical shift in consciousness, one that moves beyond identification with the body, the mind, and the ego, and opens up to the infinite potential of the universe itself. It is a journey of letting go of everything that we think we are in order to realize everything that we truly are. This is not an escape from the world but a deeper engagement with it—living with the awareness that our true nature is not separate from the universe, but an integral expression of it. In transcending the boundaries of the self, we step into a space of boundless potential, where we no longer experience life through the lens of separation and limitation, but through the lens of infinite possibility and universal connectedness. This realization of the higher dimensions of existence is, in many ways, the key to unlocking the full potential of humanity. It allows us to move beyond the narrow confines of egoism desire and fear and embrace a life of service, compassion, and love. It offers us the possibility of living in harmony with all beings, recognizing the divine presence in everything we encounter. And it shows us that the purpose of human existence is not simply to survive, to accumulate, or to compete, but to awaken to our true nature as infinite, conscious, and interconnected beings, deeply woven into the fabric of the cosmos.

Let us see a short story related to this.

Saint Francis of Assisi, born Giovanni di Pietro di Bernardone in 1181 in Italy, is one of the most beloved saints in Christian tradition, known for his radical transformation and deep spirituality. His life offers a profound example of moving beyond the egoic self, transcending the limits of the individual identity, and experiencing the divine presence in all things.

Saint Francis grew up in a wealthy family and led a carefree, indulgent life in his youth, reveling in luxury and pleasure. He was, by all accounts, a typical young man of privilege—chasing fame, material wealth, and social status. However, a deep inner dissatisfaction began to grow within him. Despite all his worldly achievements, Francis found that the pursuit of wealth and status did not bring him lasting peace or fulfillment.

This sense of emptiness intensified after he was captured and imprisoned during a war between Assisi and Perugia. It was during this time of confinement and reflection that Francis began to question the meaning of life. He felt a deep, spiritual calling that led him to abandon his former life and embrace poverty, humility, and devotion to God. He realized that the identity he had constructed around his wealth and social status was an illusion—temporary and ultimately meaningless. The "self" that he had identified with, shaped by his family, his desires, and society's expectations, was not his true essence.

One of the most defining moments in Francis's spiritual awakening occurred at San Damiano—a small church outside Assisi. One day, while praying before a crucifix, he heard the voice of Christ saying, "Francis, go and rebuild my Church." At that moment, he realized that his life's purpose was not to seek material wealth or status, but to live in service to others and to rebuild the spiritual life of the world.

This moment marked the beginning of a radical transformation, where Francis began to experience what many spiritual traditions refer to as oneness—a deep recognition of the interconnectedness of all life. His sense of separation from the world, and even from other people, dissolved as he opened himself to a profound connection with the divine presence. His faith was no longer just intellectual or doctrinal; it became a lived experience. As he embraced a life of poverty, humility, and service, Francis began to understand that the true self is not defined by the transient roles or identities we assume in society but by our divine essence, which is shared by all beings.

As Francis deepened his spiritual practice, his life began to reflect the higher dimensions of existence that the mystics speak of—states of being that transcend the ego and ordinary reality. Francis experienced what many would call mystical union with God, and in these moments, he saw all of creation as an extension of the divine. He famously referred to the sun, moon, and stars as his "brothers" and "sisters," embodying a profound sense of unity with nature.

This connection was not just intellectual or philosophical; it was deeply experiential. Francis's famous prayer, The Canticle of the Sun, expresses his recognition of the divine presence in all *aspects of nature:*

"Most High, all-powerful, good Lord, to You belong praise, glory, honor, and all blessing. To You alone, Most High, do they belong, and no man is worthy to pronounce Your name."

In this prayer, he acknowledges not only the transcendence of God but also the immanence of the divine in the world. His experience of oneness with creation went beyond mere intellectual understanding; it was a direct realization of the interconnectedness of all things.

In one of the most significant mystical experiences of his life, Saint Francis received the stigmata—the wounds of Christ—on his body. These marks, which appeared on his hands, feet, and side, symbolized his deep union with Christ and his embodiment of divine love and suffering. In this extraordinary experience, Francis's ego was utterly dissolved. He no longer saw himself as separate from Christ or from the world but became a living expression of the divine presence, embodying the very essence of love, compassion, and sacrifice.

The stigmata also symbolized a higher dimension of existence—the realm of divine unity—where the boundaries between the human and the divine, the individual and the universal, cease to exist. In this state of divine union, Francis was not merely an individual soul, but an expression of cosmic consciousness, fully attuned to the divine in all things.

As Francis continued to live out his spiritual awakening, his life became a testament to the possibility of transcending the ego and experiencing the higher dimensions of existence. He saw the poor, the sick, and the outcast as embodiments of Christ and treated them with profound love and compassion. He embraced radical selflessness, choosing a life of poverty not just for its own sake, but to dissolve the attachments of the ego and to serve the greater good.

In his later years, when his health began to fail, Francis experienced physical suffering but remained deeply peaceful, embodying the truth that his true nature was not limited by his physical body or his identity as Francis of Assisi. His essence, he understood, was one with the divine and with all creation.

In a world often consumed by individualism, competition, and material success, the story of Saint Francis of Assisi is a powerful reminder of the path beyond the self. His life shows that it is possible to transcend the limitations of the ego, to experience the higher dimensions of existence, and to live in harmony with all beings, recognizing the divine presence in everything.

Just as Saint Francis experienced oneness with creation and saw the interconnectedness of all life, the modern world, through spiritual practice, can also access these higher states of awareness. Whether through deep meditation, prayer, or acts of selfless service, individuals today can begin to move beyond the illusion of the ego and experience the infinite peace, joy, and love that lie beyond the boundaries of the personal self.

*The journey of Saint Francis embodies the idea that the purpose of human existence is not merely to survive, but to awaken to our true nature—**infinite, conscious, and interconnected with the entire cosmos**. In transcending the ego, we step into a life of service, compassion, and love, recognizing that our true essence is not separate from the universe, but an integral part of it.*

FOURTEEN

THE SOUL'S COMPASS: THE VITAL ROLE OF SPIRITUALITY IN NAVIGATING THE MODERN WORLD

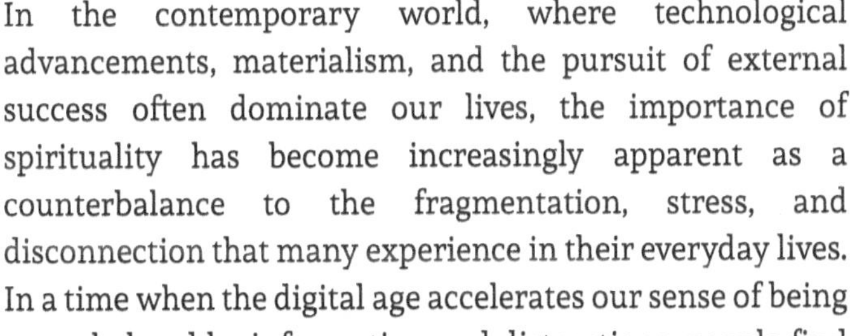

In the contemporary world, where technological advancements, materialism, and the pursuit of external success often dominate our lives, the importance of spirituality has become increasingly apparent as a counterbalance to the fragmentation, stress, and disconnection that many experience in their everyday lives. In a time when the digital age accelerates our sense of being overwhelmed by information and distractions, people find themselves grappling with a profound sense of existential crisis, loneliness, and dissatisfaction, despite living in an era of unparalleled access to resources and opportunities. Spirituality, in this context, offers a sanctuary, a deeper grounding, and a way to reconnect with the profound questions that have been at the heart of human existence for millennia: Who are we? What is the nature of life? What is our purpose in the grand scheme of the universe? Through spirituality, we begin a journey inward—a journey that leads to greater self-awareness, inner peace, and ultimately, the realization of our interconnectedness with all living beings. Spiritual practices such as meditation, prayer, mindfulness, and contemplation allow us to access a state of presence and awareness that counters the constant mental chatter and external noise of our fast-paced world. In a time when instant gratification and material pursuits are often prioritized over emotional and spiritual fulfilment, spirituality reminds us of the deeper currents of love, compassion, and wisdom that exist beneath the surface of our everyday lives. In the rush to succeed, achieve, and accumulate, the contemporary individual can easily forget the importance of developing an inner sense of peace, clarity, and connection.

Spirituality helps us break free from the cycle of ego-driven pursuits by redirecting our focus toward our true essence—the divine spark within us and our inherent connection to the universe. It invites us to move beyond the superficial layers of self-identification, which are so often shaped by societal standards, and to discover our authentic self, not as a collection of achievements or possessions, but as a limitless being interwoven with all that exists. In addition, spirituality provides tools to navigate the overwhelming emotions that can arise from living in a rapidly changing world. Mental health struggles, such as anxiety, depression, and burnout, have reached epidemic proportions in many societies, exacerbated by pressures to conform to unrealistic standards of success, beauty, and productivity. In this context, spirituality offers not only comfort and solace but also practical tools for emotional regulation, resilience, and healing. Mindfulness practices, for example, allow individuals to witness their thoughts and feelings without being consumed by them, cultivating a sense of emotional equanimity that can be a source of strength during times of adversity. Moreover, spirituality encourages a shift from an individualistic worldview to one that emphasizes interconnectedness and collective responsibility.

In a globalized world facing challenges such as climate change, social inequality, and political polarization, spirituality offers a framework for collective healing, compassion, and understanding. Many spiritual traditions, whether through meditation, prayer, or ritual, call on individuals to act in service of the greater good, to recognize the suffering of others as our own, and to work towards creating a more just and compassionate world. At its core, spirituality reminds us that the pursuit of material wealth, power, or fame is ultimately empty unless it is grounded in a deeper understanding of the intrinsic value of life, love, and kindness. In a culture that often emphasizes external validation, spirituality offers an antidote by fostering inner fulfilment and a sense of purpose that comes not from what we accumulate but from how we live and how we treat others. It is through the cultivation of virtues such as compassion, gratitude, and humility that we find true peace and lasting joy. Furthermore, as we move through the complexities of modern life, spirituality provides a sense of meaning that can be deeply transformative. While science and technology have given us the ability to manipulate the physical world, they do not necessarily provide answers to the existential questions that lie at the heart of the human experience. Spirituality, however, offers a framework for understanding the mysteries of life—why we are here, what happens after we die, and how we can live in harmony with one another and the Earth. These answers are not necessarily found in dogmatic beliefs or doctrines but through personal experience, introspection, and the willingness to explore the unseen dimensions of life that transcend the material world. In this way, spirituality becomes a path of self-discovery, not just in terms of the individual self, but in relation to the collective self—the human family, the Earth, and the cosmos.

Through spiritual practices, we learn to engage with the world not as separate entities but as interconnected expressions of the same source, fostering a sense of unity, compassion, and respect for all life. In a fragmented world that can often feel devoid of meaning, spirituality becomes a beacon of light, offering a sense of coherence and wholeness. Finally, the importance of spirituality in the contemporary world lies in its ability to provide a path toward transcendence—the experience of going beyond the ego, the limitations of the material world, and the transient nature of our individual lives. Through spiritual practice, we come to realize that we are not merely physical beings, bound by time and space, but spiritual beings with an eternal essence that connects us to the infinite. This realization can be profoundly liberating, allowing us to release the fear of death, the grip of material desires, and the pressures of societal expectations. In experiencing the transcendent, we come to know our true nature—limitless, eternal, and unconditionally connected to all that is. Thus, spirituality offers not just a remedy for the challenges of contemporary life but a pathway to the deepest freedom and fulfillment that is available to us as human beings. Through it, we awaken to our highest potential and our capacity to contribute to the greater good, not from a place of obligation but from a place of love, joy, and deep spiritual knowing.

Let us see a short story related to this.

Once, in a peaceful lake surrounded by lush green forests, two turtles lived. One was wise and cautious; the other was young and foolish. As the seasons passed, the foolish turtle grew restless, longing to see the world beyond the lake. He heard stories of the grandeur of the distant places and imagined how much more satisfying life could be outside the safety of his familiar surroundings. He eagerly persuaded his older companion to join him on a journey to explore the world. The wise turtle, aware of the dangers of the unknown, advised against leaving the lake. "There is nothing wrong with where we are. Peace and happiness can be found here if we cultivate wisdom and mindfulness. The world outside is full of uncertainty, and you may lose what you already have," the wise turtle warned. But the foolish turtle was undeterred by his friend's counsel.

One day, while the wise turtle was napping, the foolish turtle set out on his own. Along the way, he was swept into a strong wind that carried him high into the sky, far from the safety of the lake. As he travelled, he felt exhilarated at first, but soon the excitement gave way to fear and anxiety. The journey was not as thrilling as he had imagined. His heart was heavy, and he felt more lost than ever.

After a long and turbulent journey, the foolish turtle found himself in a vast, unfamiliar land. Alone and afraid, he realized that the world was not as kind or welcoming as he had thought.

Longing for the peace he had left behind, he finally returned to the lake, where the wise turtle was waiting for him.

The wise turtle welcomed him back with a smile. "**You sought the world outside, but you found only confusion and unrest. True peace does not come from external things or distant places. It resides in the heart that is calm, grounded, and connected to the present moment.**"

Conclusion: Embracing The Infinite Journey

In the end, the journey of spirituality is not about arriving at a final destination, but about embracing the on-going, infinite process of awakening to our deeper selves, our interconnectedness with the world, and the divine essence that flows through all life. To see life as a journey means recognizing that growth, transformation, and realization are not limited to any one moment but are an unfolding, ever-evolving process. The search for meaning, for self-understanding, and for truth is a path that leads us through many twists and turns, through periods of doubt, struggle, and questioning, but also through moments of clarity, joy, and profound peace. Each phase of the journey offers new lessons, new opportunities for growth, and new layers of understanding to be peeled back. To embrace the infinite journey is to accept the fact that the process of awakening never ends—there is no final, fixed state of perfection. Just as the universe itself is in a constant state of expansion and transformation, so too is the soul's journey one of perpetual evolution. At each stage, we are called to let go of the old, the outdate, and the limiting, so that we may make space for new insights, deeper awareness, and greater compassion. It is this constant unfolding, this dance of release and renewal that defines the spiritual path. The paradox of this journey is that, although it leads to a deeper understanding of the self and the universe, it also brings us to the realization that the "self" as we commonly know it is, in fact, an illusion—a transient and shifting entity that is constantly evolving. When we awaken to the truth of our deeper nature, we come to see that the infinite journey is not about achieving some idealized state or fulfilling a set of external goals, but about living with a profound awareness of the impermanence of all things, while simultaneously embracing the sacredness of the present moment. This paradox—the tension between impermanence and the sacredness of now—is the heart of spiritual practice. Whether it is through meditation, mindfulness, prayer, or simply living with greater intention and presence, every moment becomes an opportunity to realize the boundless nature of our existence, to touch the divine in the midst of the mundane, and to live in alignment with the higher dimensions of reality. The infinite journey is not a solitary path, but one that is inherently interconnected with all beings. Each step we take on this path ripples out to affect the collective consciousness, contributing to the healing, transformation, and evolution of humanity as a whole. In embracing the infinite journey, we step into a deeper sense of compassion, understanding that the suffering we encounter in the world is not separate from our own. Through this expanded awareness, we become more attuned to the needs of others, to the pain and joy that circulate through the collective experience, and to the profound interconnectedness of all life. This understanding brings with it a deep sense of responsibility—not as a burden but as a calling to live with greater love, wisdom, and service. The more we embrace the infinite journey, the more we recognize that it is not about seeking an end, but about being fully present to the journey itself. Life itself becomes the path, and every moment of experience becomes the opportunity to awaken, to serve, and to express the divine truth that resides within all of us. In this light, spirituality is not a practice reserved for certain moments or times, but a constant, living expression of who we are in the world. It is through the very act of living that we come to embody our true nature, and in doing so, we bring forth a vision of the world that is harmonious, compassionate, and deeply connected to the infinite. To walk this path is to understand that the destination is not a place but a state of being—a state of pure presence, peace, and love that we carry within us and offer to the world around us. Each individual's journey is unique, but all are threads in the same divine tapestry, each contributing to the greater whole. It is in the embrace of this infinite journey that we come to know who we truly are, not as isolated beings, but as part of an endless, interconnected dance of consciousness. We are both the travellers and the journey itself.

The ultimate truth of the spiritual path is that there is no end. The infinite journey teaches us that life is a continuous process of growth, learning, and self-discovery. It calls us to live not for a distant future or in the shadows of past regrets, but in the fullness of the present moment. The destination is not outside of us, but within. When we embrace this infinite journey, we transcend the limitations of time, space, and ego, and enter into a deeper state of being that is both timeless and expansive. In this state, we see that we are not separate from the universe, but an inseparable part of it, a living expression of the divine presence that permeates all of existence. This realization is both humbling and liberating. Humbling, because it reminds us that we are but one part of an infinite whole, and liberating because it allows us to let go of the struggle for control, the attachment to personal identity, and the fear of the unknown. The infinite journey invites us to step into the unknown with trust, to release our need for certainty, and to accept the unfolding of life as it comes. It teaches us that the process itself is the purpose, that the journey of becoming, of growing, and of awakening is where the true richness of life lies. To embrace this journey is to be alive in the truest sense—to live with an open heart, a clear mind, and a spirit that is willing to expand and evolve. The infinite journey is the journey of the soul, a journey that transcends this lifetime and extends beyond the boundaries of time, space, and physical form. It is the journey that each of us is called to walk, and in walking it, we find not only our deepest purpose but also the universal truth that we are all, in the end, one. The infinite journey is the journey of awakening to who we are, and in embracing it fully, we embrace the very essence of life itself. The path may not always be easy, but it is one that is filled with profound meaning, rich with opportunities for growth, and ultimately, a journey that leads us to the realization of our own divine nature. To embrace the infinite journey is to embrace life as it is—ever-changing, ever-evolving, and always calling us forward toward greater awareness, greater love, and greater unity. In this embrace, we find our highest calling and our deepest fulfillment.

ᏢᏢᏢ

ॐ सर्वे भवन्तु सुखिनः
सर्वे सन्तु निरामयाः।
सर्वे भद्राणि पश्यन्तु मा कश्चिद्दुःखभाग्भवेत।
ॐ शान्तिः शान्तिः शान्तिः ॐ ॥

oṃ sarve bhavantu sukhinaḥ
sarve santu nirāmayāḥ
sarve bhadrāṇi paśyantu mā kaścidduḥ khabhāgbhavetaǀ
oṃ śāntiḥ śāntiḥ śāntiḥ omǀǀ

May all sentient beings be at peace,
may no one suffer from illness,
May all see what is auspicious, may no one suffer.
Om peace, peace, peace.

Bibliography

Adhikari, T. N. (2023). *Friendly Environment in Gurukul and Psychologically Motivation of Students towards Gurukul Education. Interdisciplinary Research in Education.*

Banerjee, D., & Ray , A. (2015). *Knowledge Management: Some Theoretical Approaches. Knowledge Management.*

Bruce, A., Sheilds, L., & Molzahn, A. (2011). *Language and the (Im)possibilities of Articulating Spirituality. Journal of Holistic Nursing, 29(1), 44-52.*

Chowdhury, M., Chakraborty, A., & Chakraborty, S. (2023). *Investigating the role of workplace spirituality in promoting environmentally responsible behaviours among employees. International Journal of HRM Cases and Research, 78-88.*

Dalton, J. C. (2003). *Exploring Spirituality and Culture in Adult and Higher Education (review). Journal of College Student Development, 44(6), 861-863.*

Driscoll, C., McIsaac, E. M., & Wiebe, E. (2019). *The material nature of spirituality in the small business workplace: from transcendent ethical values to immanent ethical actions. Journal of Management, Spirituality & Religion, 16(2), 155-177.*

Duterte, J. (2024). *Rise of Organizational Spirituality in the New Normal: A Phenomenology through the Lens of HEI Leaders. International Journal of Research and Innovation in Social Science, 8(8), 4184-4190.*

Fatima, S., & Srivastava, U. (2024). *Exploring Work-Life Balance Strategies Among Generation Z In The Education Sector: An Exploratory Analysis. Educational Administration Theory and Practice journal, 30(4).*

Gaur, A. (2024). *Blending Spirituality and Leadership Abilities for Sustainable Management. OCEM Journal of Management Technology & Social Sciences, 3(2), 133-145.*

Hymn for the Weekend (2015),Song by Coldplay

Jensen, E., & Michaels, J. (2024). Religiosity and a Promotion Mindset Relate to Enhanced Meaning in Life. University of South Florida Undergraduate Research Conference.

Classic Indian Fables

Kassar, G. (2023). Exploring Cybersecurity Awareness and Resilience of SMEs amid the Sudden Shift to Remote Work during the Coronavirus Pandemic: A Pilot Study. ARPHA Conference Abstracts.

Królikowska, A. (2024). Spiritual education: Ignatian inspirations. Multidisciplinary Journal of School Education, 1(25), 13.

Marrucci, L., Daddi, T., & Iraldo, F. (2024). Creating environmental performance indicators to assess corporate sustainability and reward employees. Ecological Indicators, 158(1), 111489.

Mcguire, M. (2003). Why Bodies Matter: A Sociological Reflection on Spirituality and Materiality. Spiritus A Journal of Christian Spirituality, 3(1), 1-18.

Ohri, K., & Dutta, H. (2024). Exploring the Influence of Workplace Spirituality on Employee Engagement: A Comprehensive Literature Review. Proceedings of the 2nd International Conference on Emerging Technologies and Sustainable Business Practices-2024 (ICETSBP 2024), 206-217.

Paramartha Kathalu by Swami Vidya Prakashananda Giri Swamy

Qu, G., & Park, H. J. (2024). A Study on the Environment and Characteristics of Overtime Work in the Socialist Market Economy System of China: An Analysis from the Perspective of Marx's Labor Theory. East and West Studies, 181-216.

Quatro, S. (2004). New Age or Age Old: Classical Management Theory and Traditional Organized Religion as Underpinnings of the Contemporary Organizational

Spirituality Movement. Human Resource Development Review, 3(3), 228-249.

Sharma, K., Phrakhruvinaithorn, W., Thepa, P. A., & Patnaik, S. (2023). Implementing Mindfulness In The Workplace: A New Strategy For Enhancing Both Individual And Organizational Effectiveness. Journal for ReAttach Therapy and Developmental Diversities, 6(2), 408-416.

Yentür, D. B., & Yanmaz, K. (2023). The Effect of Employee Diversity on Organizational Performance Ethical Statement. Current Science, 5(6), 1-24.

www.ingramcontent.com/pod-product-compliance
Lightning Source LLC
Chambersburg PA
CBHW031045160726
47991CB00005B/2029